MOUNTAIN OF SECRETS

A LEGACY THRILLER

MOUNTAIN OF SECRETS

DARCY MCDANIEL

Mountain of Secrets

Copyright © 2024 by Darcy McDaniel.

All rights reserved.

No part of this publication may be reproduced, distributed, or transmitted in any form or by any means, including photocopying, recording, or other electronic or mechanical methods, without the prior written permission of the author, except as permitted by U.S. copyright law.

Cover Image: Generated by DALL·E

Book Formatting: Derek Murphy of Creativindie

Editor: Mike Waitz of Sticks and Stones Freelance Editing

Publisher: Sinlahekin Publishing LLC

The story and all names, characters, and incidents portrayed are fiction and products of the author's imagination. No identification with actual persons, living or deceased, places, or events is intended or should be inferred.

ISBN: 979-8-9905282-0-8

First Edition: May 2024

Printed in the United States of America

9 79 89 90 52 82 08

For my family, the driving force behind these pages.

CONTENTS

CHAPTER ONE	1
CHAPTER TWO	14
CHAPTER THREE	26
CHAPTER FOUR	39
CHAPTER FIVE	61
CHAPTER SIX	72
CHAPTER SEVEN	91
CHAPTER EIGHT	106
CHAPTER NINE	128
CHAPTER TEN	145
CHAPTER ELEVEN	162
CHAPTER TWELVE	178
CHAPTER THIRTEEN	194
CHAPTER FOURTEEN	208
ACKNOWLEDGMENTS	232
ABOUT THE AUTHOR	233

ONE

From Hell to Breakfast

"LET'S GO, SIERRA!" Ruth LaRae shouted at her younger sister. The sharp sound echoed through the rocky canyons and timbered slopes of their summer grazing pasture. "The cows have scattered from hell to breakfast." A low-lying branch from a fir tree slapped Sierra, snapping her back to reality as she hustled to the front to turn the herd.

"That will leave a mark," Sierra said under her breath. Her horse, Lucky, a magnificent palomino with a flaxen mane, chomped at his bit, eager to run. Sierra shared Lucky's love for speed and pushing the limits. Tall and athletic, Sierra's six-foot stature towered over her older sister, Ruth, who resembled their mother, Penny, in both height and resilience. What she lacked in height, Ruth made up for in grit.

While the mid-day sun illuminated Cathedral Canyon, Sierra's black and gray timber wolf tattoo danced in the sunlight on her left arm, her long blonde braid swaying from side to side as Lucky strolled behind the cows. Viking alt-cowboy was her self-described style, which was a far cry from the sea of Carhartt and flannel in rural Wyoming.

"All right, Sierra. Let's hold them up here," Ruth said as she pointed to the meadow about thirty yards ahead. Once they had moved the herd to the meadow, Ruth dismounted her horse, Buck, and rifled through her saddlebag. The supple leather melted under her fingers and the smell of saddle butter lingered from greasing her saddle the day before.

Deep in the backcountry, technology met tradition head-on as Ruth pulled a drone from her saddlebag. While Sierra challenged viewpoints through self-expression, Ruth preferred transcending limitations through innovation. The ranching community challenged Ruth's willingness to use technology to bolster efficiency, despite its proven advantages. Most people were resistant to change, but Wyoming locals could exhibit an even stronger reluctance.

"I'll fly the timber for stragglers and then check the fences," Ruth said while preparing the drone for flight. She unzipped the case, unfolded the arms, inserted the battery, and powered on the remote controller and drone. After she positioned the landing pad, she waited for a GPS signal to activate the obstacle detection. Once powered on, the humming sound cleared any grasshoppers lurking in the area. In less than a couple of minutes, the drone was airborne and buzzed above. With about three hundred cattle in the pasture, counting them could be difficult, and the LaRaes sought any advantage in the backcountry. Ruth and Sierra's younger brother, Luke, suggested the idea of using a drone since it was more efficient than him flying his Piper Super Cub airplane. Using the drone made quick work of an all-day job.

The drone also provided a bird's-eye view from above and a means to explore deep within the rugged landscape, revealing items hidden by vegetation or concealed by topography. Some locations, like the Arthur McCray place, were tough to access, though flying the drone overhead evened the playing field. Locals speculated on the history of the area and how the LaRaes ended up with the Arthur McCray homestead surrounding Cathedral Canyon: an area that is a significant part of the LaRaes' ranch. Arthur McCray mysteriously disappeared, leaving no clues behind, but their Great-Grandpa Lee LaRae took over his homestead, which stoked suspicion. Cathedral Canyon had a special meaning to the LaRae family for reasons the sisters were only now piecing together.

As the drone scanned the landscape, Ruth discovered more cattle. "Looks like ten plus kegged up by Willie's Rock." When she finished flying over the timber, she picked up speed before transitioning to checking the fences. "With the fence down south of Willie's Rock, we can repair it on our way up." Ruth swapped out the battery and finished covering the ground as the drone sailed through the air. After selecting "Return to Home" on her remote controller, she landed the drone back in the meadow. The lush green meadow made a striking contrast with the gray plastic drone that looked more like a giant insect than a technological marvel. Although it seemed out of place, it was the perfect way to bridge the gap between technology and ranching.

MOUNTAIN OF SECRETS

After Ruth powered off the drone and remote controller, she looked around the meadow. She chuckled while imagining the early homesteaders seeing a drone in the pasture. *Modern tools and forgotten ways intertwined in Wyoming's wilds.* Once she packed up the drone and returned it to her saddlebag, she climbed back in her saddle. "Listo," Ruth said to Sierra, who nodded, and they made their way to Willie's Rock to fix the fence and gather the stragglers. Ruth had been brushing up on her Spanish to prepare for a trip to Mexico in the fall. Birds chirped from the aspen stand as the steady breeze ruffled the vibrant green leaves.

About an hour later, they arrived at the first fence repair. Sierra grabbed the fencing pliers from her saddlebag and the stretcher secured to her saddle. She walked over to the fence to pull the wires taut and splice them back together again. Strong from ranch work, she ratcheted the stretcher with ease.

She unwound the barbed wire ends, made a v-shape, interlocked and twisted the strands to secure the splice, then repeated for the second wire. Sierra breezed through the repair job of two broken wires on a five-wire fence. She put her foot in the stirrup, grabbed the saddle horn, and pulled herself up in one graceful motion. Soon, they resumed their journey to Willie's Rock in search of the rest of the herd.

While riding through the timber, picking their route to avoid blowdown, a chipmunk chattered, warning the others of danger. They were close to Willie's Rock, and they hit the opening in the timber before zigzagging through large boulders. "I have six over here," Sierra said, gesturing over her left shoulder. Ruth rode ahead to look for the others. She counted five more before she moved toward an opening in the timber.

Ruth felt she needed to fly over the area again and grabbed her drone from her saddlebag. Once she was airborne, she scanned the timber floor and openings for cattle. It wasn't even five minutes into her flight before she found three more.

"There are more cattle north of here in the next opening." Ruth fixated on the display screen of the remote controller. "Sierra," she said, blinking rapidly, "I think I found a wooden cross marking a grave."

"Are you serious?" Sierra approached her location on Lucky.

"Yes," Ruth said, with a deadpan expression washing over her face.

When Ruth positioned the drone for a closer look, the low battery warning began beeping on her remote controller. She captured photos of the wooden cross and took a waypoint, then rushed back to land. "Ruth, what's going on?"

"My battery is almost dead; I need to land right away."

"Now I'm curious," Sierra said, watching her sister maneuver the drone. Sierra noticed Ruth needed to concentrate on making a precision landing, yet she found herself intrigued by the wooden cross. The remote controller was beeping more steadily, alerting Ruth to the urgency of the situation. Leaves kicked up from the ground as the drone descended onto the landing pad. With only moments to spare, she positioned the drone right on target.

"It's my final battery for the drone and the remote controller is low on battery life, too. We'll need to revisit this discovery later at the house."

With a sidelong glance, Sierra turned toward Ruth. "Oh, the suspense unfolding here at Cathedral Canyon."

After preparing the drone for transport, Ruth returned to the saddle. "That was an unexpected find."

"Did it look like an old-fashioned cross?"

"Yes, and I could distinguish some words, Arthur Mc-something."

"Interesting. I remember Dad mentioning Arthur McCray as part of the first homesteaders in the McGrath Valley. Now we find a wooden cross." Sierra's words lingered and there was an awkward silence between the sisters before Ruth interjected.

"I'll grab the cattle and bring them back here."

Sierra could sense Ruth's discomfort about the subject and that she needed some space.

"Okay, I'll be here." Sierra bit her tongue. She wanted to quiz Ruth about the wooden cross, but resisted the urge as she watched Buck trot up the slope. The afternoon sun exposed every opening in the tree canopy and creatures scurrying across the forest floor. About twenty minutes later, Ruth returned with eight more head of cattle and joined them with Sierra's bunch, and they made their way back to the meadow. Sierra shivered while glancing at Ruth. The silence during the ride back was eerie, tension thick in the air.

As Ruth and Sierra spotted the main herd in the tree-lined meadow, the strain eased between them. Ruth squinted from the sun as the small bunch joined the rest of the herd during the hottest part of the day. Sierra smacked her lips and commented on having a dry mouth. The two women sipped from their canteens, contemplating the day's events and the history of the wooden cross. Next, they dismounted and led their horses to a galvanized steel stock water tank, and then grabbed a quick bite of food from their saddlebags. The afternoon sunlight irradiated Ruth's flushed cheeks. "Vamonos," Ruth said, while she swung her leg over the saddle as Buck swatted the flies with his tail.

While the sisters left the herd and made their way to the pickup point, Ruth's wavy auburn locks were in a loose side braid, wispy strands highlighting her high cheekbones as she sat back in the saddle on her beloved buckskin, Buck. Honest like the day was long, Buck was Paul's—her father's horse.

In 2013, one week before Ruth's eighteenth birthday, tragedy struck the LaRae family. Paul and Penny LaRae died in a car crash while returning from Jacks, Wyoming, during a snowstorm. Their white Ford F-150 hit a stretch of black ice, skidded into a guardrail, then spun one hundred and eighty degrees into oncoming traffic, where a semi-truck hit them head-on. Their death rocked the small ranching community of Telford for years to come. Although each child dealt with the trauma differently, they grew closer.

Ruth took the loss of her parents the hardest. The eldest LaRae child, Ruth, was a true overachiever. She excelled in athletics, academics, and extracurricular activities, and earned a full-ride academic scholarship to Washington State University, one of the leading veterinary schools. Her dream was to become a large-animal vet and start a practice in Telford. However, after the accident, Ruth cared for her siblings and the ranch. She never looked back or second guessed her decision. The fear of disappointing her family stayed with her, driving her to work harder than ever before.

MOUNTAIN OF SECRETS

As the fourth generation, Ruth didn't just take over her family ranch. She carried on a legacy. Homesteaded in 1883 by her Great-Grandpa Lee LaRae, the 2L Ranch had been a staple in the McGrath Valley. The sprawling ranch encompassed 3,600 acres of pristine land ideal for hunting and grazing. With creeks, lakes, and ponds and granite boulders, timbered slopes, and mountain meadows, the views were as complex and varied as the wildlife with frequent deer, elk, moose, lynx, and a variety of birds.

There were layers of intrigue, as nature intended. This lifestyle, with more substance than superficial aspects, embraced values from family to caring for the land and animals, and an unspoken bond that brought it all together. The connection to the land was hard to describe. It was more than a place; it was a way of life. For Ruth and her siblings, it was in their blood. Steeped in history and sacrifice, there were no limits for the LaRaes to protect their family legacy. Nate Teague, their archenemy, lurked in the shadows, but they were determined not to let him stand in their way.

With the clicking of horseshoes over rocks, the sisters focused on the horizon. The fringe on their chaps flapped in the breeze like fishing lures, trying to catch the wind. "I'll never forget the call from Grandma Sally." Ruth's voice quivered as she gripped the reins a little tighter. "Cathedral Canyon brings back a lot of memories. It's been ten years since the accident, but it still feels like yesterday."

As Ruth's words hung in the air, the intense summer sun retreated behind the craggy peaks with bright orange, red, and purple hues painting the skies above. When the light waned, the canyon came to life with small animals scampering across downed logs and owls hooting from the tree canopy. A lone wolf let out a mournful howl that drowned out the background noise. Buck's and Lucky's eyes and ears darted around as they continued making their way to the pickup point, where Luke waited with the truck and trailer.

"Dad proposed to Mom in Alfred Meadows, over by the creek. I wish they could see us holding down the ranch."

"Seeing our heritage live on, wild as ever, would make them proud," Ruth said, wiping her brow.

In unison, Sierra and Ruth said, "Cowgirls don't cry. Because Wyoming is too rough for delicate flowers." Words they had heard countless times from their father. At six foot three, Paul LaRae was a formidable man, and he instilled strength and courage in his daughters and reminded them they were every bit as capable as any man. Paul was progressive yet pragmatic and wanted nothing more than for his children to be self-sufficient, especially his two daughters.

While growing up, the youngest of four, Paul had worked alongside his three older sisters on the 2L Ranch. Wyoming history documented their forward-thinking viewpoints as Louisa Swain, a distant relative, became the first woman to vote in Wyoming, with the Women's Suffrage Law in 1869, twenty-one years before Wyoming became a state. Paul often boasted to his children the LaRaes had always been at the forefront.

Paul and Penny dedicated themselves to teaching their children a variety of skills without reference to gender traditions. They could hunt, fish, weld, run a chainsaw, and split gears on a 13-speed as well as they could cook, sew, and do laundry. Their parents hailed Ruth for her mechanical skills, Sierra for her marksmanship, and Luke for his flying. Both daughters received awards in welding, shooting sports, lumber sports, and cooking competitions. Luke bought his first airplane with money he received from developing an app for pilots and he has been a top contender in chuckwagon cookouts. Paul and Penny joked they might have taken raising independent and capable children a little too far.

Ruth and Sierra harkened their parents' words and support, adopting them into a personal credo, *Anything and Everything*. True to their nature, Ruth restored a '67 Mustang and donated the proceeds to local charities, including a no-kill animal shelter, PAWS of Jacks. Sierra, despite two broken ribs, showcased her grit and resilience, as the runner-up in a Canadian Wilderness Challenge.

Drawing inspiration from his sisters' ethos, Luke LaRae pursued his passion for flying. The youngest of the three, with a five-year age gap between him and Ruth, Luke shared their drive and determination. Standing tall at six foot two, with sandy blonde hair, brilliant blue eyes, and a killer smile, he was popular with women, though he was far from ready to settle down. Like his older sisters, Luke possessed tremendous motivation. He earned his pilot's license before he could drive a car and preferred flying to driving any day. His loyalty to his sisters knew no bounds; he would do anything for them.

Rather than pursuing a career as a fighter pilot flying F-16s, Luke stayed in Wyoming. He loved the ranch and his sisters, but he longed to be in the air.

Born with wings, Luke enjoyed the exhilaration of soaring through the clouds. When he wasn't navigating the skies, he devoted himself to keeping the family ranch thriving. Like his mother, he enjoyed tending to the business affairs of the ranch. Channeling his mother's expertise as a licensed accountant, Luke started helping Ruth with the books when he was only thirteen. With the fluctuating nature of commercial cattle prices, he proposed leveraging their hunting and guiding skills, as well as their local knowledge, to start an outfitter business to supplement their income. Luke took charge of the day-to-day operations for LaRae Outfitters, and his keen business sense and personable nature helped establish the company as one of the top three outfitters in western Wyoming.

Since the outfitter business was seasonal, Luke helped his sisters with the cattle, haying, and other activities on the ranch. He also delivered supplies by plane to locals in the McGrath Valley. Luke's versatility and willingness to pitch in wherever needed were invaluable to the family's operations.

Ruth, a natural leader, ran the ranch and all things associated with the LaRaes. She inherited her dad's planning and logistic skills and was a fierce task manager, according to her siblings. Her steady leadership guided the smooth running of the ranch while Sierra, artistic by nature, managed the marketing aspects of selling their organic beef and promoting their outfitter business. Though quiet and humble, Sierra was far more adept than she let on.

In the face of tragedy, the LaRae siblings had grown closer than ever, realizing their survival and continuing their family legacy depended on it.

As the daylight faded, they approached the pickup point. "Fancy seeing you here," Ruth said as Luke flashed the headlights on his gray Chevy Duramax.

MOUNTAIN OF SECRETS

With a big smile, Luke said, "I have nowhere else to be." Two months ago, Luke had crashed his Super Cub while flying into a remote area to check the game cameras for his outfitter business. The plane suffered a mechanical issue mid-air that resulted in a crash landing. Luke walked away with a broken arm and several lacerations, though the crash totaled his prized Super Cub and accrued more emotional baggage than he cared to admit.

An investigation revealed that a disconnected fuel line caused the mishap. Luke could replace the plane with insurance, but he couldn't forget the incident or finding the person responsible for it. Nate Teague, his nemesis, had a hand in the crash, though he couldn't prove it…yet. Like a mountain lion hunting his prey, Luke would strike at the perfect moment.

As Luke grappled with the aftermath of the plane mishap and sought to uncover the truth, his calmness acted like a steady beacon, supporting his sisters whenever they needed help. Without missing a beat, he walked back and unlatched the gate on their Wilson aluminum gooseneck trailer. Ruth and Sierra dismounted their horses and loosened their cinches. Next, they led Buck and Lucky into the trailer, then secured their reins before closing the gate. When they climbed into the truck, Gus, a three-legged border collie, greeted them and wagged his tail excitedly. Luke and Sierra exchanged glances as they slammed the truck doors shut, Lainey Wilson's "Wildflowers and Wild Horses" playing on the radio.

Once the LaRaes left the area, the trailer clearance lights popped against the darkness of night, the rails glistening like a Christmas light show winding through the bends of Badger Mountain Road. "Luke," Sierra said, lifting her gaze. "We found a wooden cross today with the drone." Luke almost swerved off the road before he collected himself.

"Where?"

Ruth studied Luke's face, trying to gauge his reaction. "North of Willie's Rock. The name Arthur and a last name starting with Mc were discernible. Arthur McCray homesteaded the area near Cathedral Canyon, though I know little about him or his story."

"There is plenty more to learn about Arthur McCray," Luke said with a loud sigh.

Now biting her lip, Sierra connected the dots. "You mean you already knew about this, Luke?"

"Yes, Dad made me promise not to say anything about the wooden cross or Arthur McCray until one of us discovered it."

"Well," Ruth said, "it sounds like we have a lot to talk about."

"Yes, yes, we do," Luke said as the headlights pierced through the pitch-black night. The drive back to the ranch was quiet as the discovery of the wooden cross weighed heavily on their minds.

Ruth sat back and folded her arms. *What else aren't we telling each other?*

TWO

By Hook or By Crook

IT FELT LIKE a pressure cooker inside Luke's truck. The air was rife with apprehension after finding the wooden cross and Luke having prior knowledge of it.

"All right, Luke," Ruth said. "Let's put the horses away and pick this up in the morning after we've had some sleep."

Even though he felt guilty about keeping the secret, he had made a promise to his dad—the last promise he ever made to him. His dad told him that after discovering the wooden cross, the other pieces would fall into place. Luke didn't know the details, but he trusted his father's judgment. *Dad was always a meticulous planner*, Luke thought, *so there must be a reason for his approach, even if it doesn't make sense yet.*

Luke bit his cheek while backing the trailer in near the barn. Ruth and Sierra unlatched the trailer gate, unloaded their horses, removed the saddles and saddle blankets, and then led Buck and Lucky to the pasture. A light breeze stirred through the meadow as Luke set out fresh hay for the horses and checked their water. The smell of sweat and leather wafted through the barn. Soon, it would be daylight and the LaRaes needed to rest up after a long day.

Trixie, a sweet-natured Siamese barn cat, purred and rubbed against Sierra's leg. She knelt and picked her up. After watching her with Trixie, Ruth's eyes scanned the horizon.

Sierra placed Trixie on a straw bale in the barn before returning to the main house. From the front door, Luke and Ruth waved back to Sierra. The events at Cathedral Canyon weighed heavily on her mind, bringing painful truths to light. Sierra harbored her own secret at Lake Louisa that her siblings didn't know the full story about. She knew she needed to tell them, but she also grappled with the secret her dad shared with her about their past. Sierra paced on the porch as haunting memories of Lake Louisa flooded in.

Meanwhile, inside the house, Ruth looked around and smacked the beam. She admired the craftsmanship, her fingernails tapping the wood. Although original to the homestead, the main house was two smaller homes joined together by her Great-Grandpa Lee Marshall LaRae in 1889. Lee, an adept adventurer, could do anything.

Despite only a third-grade education, Lee left New Brunswick aboard a boat headed for New York when he was thirteen to meet up with his sister. After New York, Lee took on odd jobs, including working on a riverboat in the Deep South before heading west, with the North Star guiding him on his adventures. He navigated many extremes as he traveled the country.

It was rather circumstantial how he landed in Wyoming. After getting bucked off a horse and breaking his leg, he stayed the winter of 1882, rather than continuing his journey north. The appeal of western Wyoming resonated with Lee. A year later, he homesteaded in the McGrath Valley. Before the winter of 1888, he settled down with a strong-willed woman, Lucy Conrad. With Lucy by his side, he enjoyed working the land and blazing his trail. Lee was intelligent, from juggling business ventures to learning languages to writing poetry, and he was quick to lend a helping hand. Long ago, people measured integrity by a man's word: Lee's word was priceless.

Ruth dusted off an old family album from the bookshelf and began looking through the photos. She might find more clues from the photos of Arthur McCray. Ruth studied a photo of her Great-Grandpa Lee and Great-Grandma Lucy in front of the barn that still stands today. In the McGrath Valley, Lee and Lucy lived a full life with their two children, Sig and Emma. Lee passed away from a sudden illness when Sig was thirteen. Sig took over the ranch when he was eighteen, and he later married an artist, Sally Worthers. With three daughters and one son, Sig and Sally forged ahead. After a massive stroke in his 70s, Sig passed away. Soon after, his son, Paul, took over running the ranch.

Despite Sig and Sally having maintained the homestead and performed modest updates, Paul and Penny completed an extensive remodel, including new buildings. Because of the remodel's size, Paul obtained his general contractor license to reduce costs. He also planned the remodel in stages to match the seasons and workload.

The ranch, rich in history, inspired Paul and Penny to maintain the family heritage, yet modernize the ranch to support future generations. Additional upgrades and improvements favored efficiency, including a hydraulic cattle chute, panels, and farming equipment. It took three years to finish the extensive renovation, including the main house, guesthouse, and shop, surpassing projections by six months because of an early snow. From Sally's art, Sig's cowboy hat, and Lee's spurs, to Lucy's shotgun, the main house was a tribute to those who came before with room for those who came next.

Ruth looked around at the house with a sense of nostalgia after going through the old family photos as she walked upstairs. Before drifting off to sleep, the gentle sound of wind chimes lingering from the porch filled her room.

✶ ✶ ✶

While the sun rose from the tree-capped ridgeline surrounding the main house, its rays shimmered across the meadow. The morning felt invigorating for the LaRae siblings as they watched a herd of deer graze nearby. Unamused with the deer, the horses trotted off as the meadowlarks sang an enchanting melody. After returning from chores, they walked inside with a hint of apprehension. Sierra invited everyone to sit, pulling out chairs in the kitchen as she handed out slices of piping hot banana bread she had put in the oven before they headed outside.

With everyone seated, Ruth grabbed the memory card from the drone and displayed the footage on her laptop. "Luke and Sierra, look at what we found," she said, scrolling to the photos of the wooden cross. She zoomed in on one photo, revealing the faint but legible hand-carved name "Arthur McCray" and the year "1888." Ruth broke the ice in her usual cut-to-the-chase manner. "How about telling us the story about the wooden cross?"

Luke took a long exhale and puffed his cheeks. The air hissed as it crossed his lips. "Let's start at the beginning." Ruth and Sierra were quiet, and watched Luke's demeanor. "When I was thirteen, I went with Dad to fix the fence near Willie's Rock. He mentioned that while I was flying airplanes, I might uncover something buried with time. Those were his exact words. I pressed Dad for more information." His sisters leaned in slightly, eager to hear more.

Tapping his fingers on the table, Luke shared Great-Grandpa Lee's story as told to Grandpa Sig and passed down to his father. Luke mentioned their dad didn't tell everything to all his children. He wanted each child to play a role in sharing their family history and working together.

By setting the stage, Luke began recalling the events. Since 1883, there was bad blood between Great-Grandpa Lee and Arthur McCray. Even though they were neighbors, they couldn't be further apart. To achieve his goals, Arthur showed no mercy. And when Great-Grandpa Lee and Arthur McCray were courting the same woman, Lucy Conrad, Arthur decided there wasn't room enough for him and Lee in the McGrath Valley. Despite Lucy making it known that Lee had her heart, Arthur had other plans.

To settle things, Arthur challenged Great-Grandpa Lee to a long-range target match in the fall of 1888, and the loser of the competition would leave behind the McGrath Valley and Lucy Conrad. Target matches were a Sunday staple for highfalutin folks and were popular well before organized sports. However, this event wasn't for sport but spite with higher stakes. Arthur suggested the winner would be whoever could hit the target three times, with the closest grouping near the center of the target from one hundred yards. Afterward, the defeated would sign over his land, say goodbye to Lucy, and vacate.

Great-Grandpa Lee suspected Arthur, his intentions, and whether he would honor the agreement. Against his better judgment, he agreed to the terms, but with one condition: He picked the location. Arthur approved without incident, which surprised him. Although he sensed a shift in Arthur's behavior, he couldn't pinpoint the cause. As part of their agreement, they decided to settle their differences through a long-range target shooting match. They scheduled it for high noon the next day.

Luke paused and looked around the room. "Before he came to Wyoming, Dad mentioned Great-Grandpa Lee lived a different life. He carried a gun and avoided answering the door at night for a reason." Ruth and Sierra hung on to Luke's every word; captivated by his retelling of a story they had not heard before. Where there was one secret, there were more, and Ruth kept a family secret of her own.

There had always been an air of mystery surrounding

Great-Grandpa Lee, and Ruth's mind raced with possibilities. Like an outlaw who lived in the shadows and followed the North Star, he traveled many miles under the cover of darkness.

"Keep going, Luke."

"Okay," Luke said as he took a drink of water. "I might need something more potent than water for what comes next." With a bottle of whiskey in his hand, Luke poured three glasses and handed them out. All three raised their glasses and exchanged glances.

Luke set down his drink and picked up where he left off in the story. The glass rocked on the table before he steadied it with his palm. "Great-Grandpa Lee selected the area we call Alfred Meadows, where we placed the stock water tank. He used a large fir tree at one hundred yards to display the target made from a gunnysack with a hand-drawn 'X' in charcoal from a wood fire. Two nails pounded into the tree would hold the gunnysack against the fir tree. However, he expected the action to happen before they arrived at the tree and somewhere near the bluffs."

After another sip of whiskey, Luke reflected as he traced the rim with his fingers. "He picked the location by the fir tree because he was prepared for a trap and wanted to leverage his familiarity with the area to his advantage. Arthur would likely position himself above the bluffs to have an unobstructed view of the meadow and his rival traveling his usual route from the south. Yet, Great-Grandpa Lee had devised a plan to approach from the west, taking advantage of the dense timber and large boulders for concealment. He would have the surprise advantage, *not* Arthur."

While Lee decided his first instinct was his best, he prepared his Winchester Model 1886 .45-70 lever action for the next day. He cleaned the barrel and polished the stock, wiping five hand-carved tally marks, and for a contingency, he readied his Colt Model 1849 Pocket Revolver. Lee sharpened his hunting knife, too. Arthur would bring his Winchester Model 1873 .44-40 rifle, though Lee didn't know what else.

"After a restless night, Great-Grandpa Lee walked out to the corral overlooking the meadow and craggy peaks. While clutching Lucy's photo, he remembered his purpose and the stakes. In the corral stood Maggie, a sturdy-built bay mare. I can picture this scene, so I embellished it a little," Luke said with his eyes twinkling.

Lee packed light with only the essentials, including his rifle, revolver, binos, shovel, hunting knife, two small boards, smooth wire, and a flask. He rubbed his mustache between his thumb and index finger as he scanned the valley. The morning, still and crisp, belied the emotions running through his head.

When he secured the items, he threw his leg over the saddle, pulled himself up, and rode off to the rendezvous point minus his land patent. By hook or by crook, he would be victorious.

Luke remembered another detail from his father. It was a brisk mid-September morning in 1888. Winter was knocking on the door. The sun peeked over the mountains as Maggie covered the ground with ease. It was a beautiful morning. Wyoming in all its glory. As Great-Grandpa Lee navigated the surroundings, he hugged the treeline to stay hidden.

Maggie tensed up and took a wide berth around a pack of wolves feasting on an elk carcass.

Beyond the wolves, an opening appeared in the timber. He used it to survey the area. With two hours left, he was past halfway, and he and Maggie continued. The tranquil morning and chilly mountain air made the ride refreshing. A slight breeze flowed through the aspens, rustling the leaves that flickered against the sunlight. Since he left at dawn, the sun now approached its highest point in the sky. With an hour to go, Great-Grandpa Lee tied the reins to a tree as he approached a boulder outcropping. Before he left, he took a swig from the flask and grabbed his binos, knife, and rifle. He licked the whiskey from his mustache as he assessed the boulders and planned his route.

His nimble fingers clutched the boulders, and within minutes, he was out of sight as he went deeper into the forest. From a small opening, he glassed the surrounding area. As he suspected, his binos caught the glare of a rifle barrel to the south along the bluffs. Although he was too far away for a shot, he continued taking cover in the mountains and inched closer to Arthur. The tree branches brushed against his torso as he sneaked up toward Arthur.

Now his breathing was deep and controlled, and every move was deliberate. He steadied his rifle with the sights on Arthur and acknowledged him. Arthur whirled and began shooting. Without hesitation, he fired his prized Winchester Model 1886 and hit Arthur with one shot to the chest. Arthur fell to the ground and landed on his back. With an abundance of caution, Lee stepped closer, his rifle drawn, ready to fire again if needed. The bullet entry, marked by a red circle on

Arthur's once-white shirt, radiated from his chest. He knelt to check his pulse. Arthur was gone.

Next, he went through Arthur's pockets and found the land patent with a note addressed to him. A sweet stench emanated from Arthur, like someone who wasn't well. He read the note: "Take good care of my place and my horse, Charlie. I knew it would end this way, but I wanted you to earn it. Signed Arthur." Lee became misty-eyed as he put the land patent and note in his pocket and went looking for Arthur's horse. Charlie was a striking, dapple-gray gelding. He could see him tied to a tree about seventy yards away. Lee retrieved Charlie and hurled Arthur over the saddle.

Rifle in one hand, he headed back to Maggie, holding the reins in the other. He would bury Arthur in the boulder outcropping where it was almost impossible to access. Once he arrived, he eased Arthur to the ground. Lee walked back with Charlie to Maggie along the narrow edge to grab the shovel from behind his saddle and the two small boards, and the smooth wire from his saddlebag. While catching his breath, he tied Charlie's reins to an adjacent tree. He placed his rifle in the scabbard after adding another tally with his knife, and headed back to the boulder outcropping. For a somber moment, he ran his fingers over the carvings, thinking about the person each mark represented.

Once he finished digging the grave, he lowered Arthur below. After he paid his respects, he filled the grave back in with dirt. The sound of a shovel clanking against rocks filled the canyon. Next, he carved "ARTHUR MCCRAY" on the first board and "1888" on the second. Lee then positioned the boards into a cross secured by smooth wire and anchored by large rocks.

Before returning to the horses, Great-Grandpa Lee gathered his shovel and cast a last glance around. He felt relieved one battle had ended, but he knew there would be others. Birds chirped and chipmunks chattered as the emptiness of Cathedral Canyon lifted. Once he arrived at the horses, Maggie nuzzled him as he stroked her mane. He was dripping in sweat and smudged with dirt. It was a solemn trip back home. The gentle breeze soothed his nerves. One month later, he proposed to Lucy, and she accepted his proposal, and so began the 2L Ranch legacy.

"Until his last day, Great-Grandpa Lee kept the events of that day a secret, only sharing them with his son, Sig. He wanted us to show reverence for this place to honor its past and future."

"Wow, I did not expect to hear that, Luke."

He found it odd how Ruth enunciated each word.

"As Dad used to say, we live on the fringe. Caught in between two worlds. Although we can't have the light without the dark, we choose which prevails. Pioneers were a different breed. There is a certain edge that comes from putting everything on the line. By doing whatever it takes."

While Luke let those words soak in, Ruth glanced at her siblings with a furrowed brow. "Are there more graves?"

Sierra struggled to sit still, fidgeting and tapping her foot on the floor. Ruth sniffed out her nervousness and fixated on Sierra.

Now wringing her hands, Sierra took a deep breath. She mentioned their dad had divided the secrets among them.

He wanted to avoid anyone knowing all of them. "So, we had to work together," she said as her pitch grew a couple of octaves. "He made me promise I wouldn't divulge my secret until Luke shared his." A pained look swept over her.

"How many more?"

"At least one, Ruth." Sierra gulped, as if swallowing her emotions.

With a wry smile, Luke turned to Sierra, and placed his hand on her shoulder. "Sierra," he said in a slow, smooth drawl, "don't keep us waiting too long."

The disclosure about Arthur McCray hit Ruth cold, like a snowstorm in July. Luke's recounting of the story made it tangible. The veins in Ruth's forehead protruded as a blank stare settled on her face. With the LaRaes having one of the largest ranches in western Wyoming, they were ascending a mountain of secrets. Sierra's revelation of another body served as a stark reminder: they were committed.

THREE

Fight Tooth and Nail

AFTER AN EMOTIONAL morning of unearthing family secrets, it was almost noon. Sierra gazed at the meadow, transported to another era. "Sierra, are you with us?"

"Yes, I'm back now."

Ruth put her rough, callused hand on Sierra's chiseled shoulder. "Do you need some time?"

"I'm ready to tell the story," Sierra said after a long pause while shifting in her chair. "When I was sixteen, Dad and I were installing a new galvanized steel stock water tank in Alfred Meadows after someone shot up the existing one. Although Ruth and I suspected it was the two oldest Allen boys, we couldn't prove it. I remember the morning was nippy with a light dew and the sun's rays felt amazing. With a serious expression, Dad informed me about something concerning our family.

"He mentioned he needed the three of us to work together after he passed. I paused while I collected my thoughts, and Dad motioned for me to follow him as he walked toward the trees surrounding the meadow. I joined him, and I'll never forget what Dad told me next." She rested her hands in her lap with her timber wolf tattoo on full display.

Sierra traced her forearm with her fingernails. "I remember Dad telling the story like it was yesterday." When Great-Grandpa Lee homesteaded the 2L Ranch in 1883, he had to fight tooth and nail to hold on to it. From bone-chilling cold to blistering heat to personal hardships to marauding plunderers, Great-Grandpa Lee and Great-Grandma Lucy had many challenges to contend with here in the McGrath Valley. To protect the ranch and his family, nothing was off limits, including murder.

Dad reached out to the largest fir tree as if making a grand gesture. Stout and imposing, the giant fir stood out among the rest. The tree served as a last stop for rustlers, who took their final breath while hanging from its hefty branches. "It sounds like it was the same tree that Great-Grandpa Lee wanted to designate as the marker tree in the long-range target shooting competition with Arthur McCray."

Luke raised his eyebrows and looked at her. "I can see that, Sierra. It's a massive tree."

The large fir tree played a pivotal role in addressing thieves. Cattle rustling almost wiped out the 2L Ranch. In the fall of 1890, Great-Grandpa Lee caught rustlers with one hundred head of his cattle. At first, he tried going through the legal system. However, it became apparent evidence influenced the county judge's decision less than money did.

Soon he realized the county judge was a strange bedfellow with anyone with deep pockets, so Great-Grandpa Lee needed a different approach. He could either treat the symptom or attack the problem. After opting for the latter, he organized a small group of local ranchers. They needed little convincing to band together in combating these offenses.

In the spring of 1891, he assembled the Night Riders, acknowledging that while the ranches were most vulnerable during the summer months, they could come under attack without warning at any time of year. After their formation, the Night Riders caught rustlers red-handed with sixty head of cattle. Through some persuasive techniques, the local ranchers discovered the bunch worked with an associate of Albert Bothwell, one of the most ruthless cattle barons in Wyoming.

While assessing the herd, they found that the sixty cattle, branded on their right sides, came from two Night Riders' herds. They captured the rustlers before they could rebrand the herd. Most thieves used a running iron, a metal O-ring that, once heated, could form most brands. Although there weren't any cattle with the 2L brand, two horses stood out.

Once closer, Great-Grandpa Lee recognized Betty and Colt. Betty, the shiny black mare, was his wife's horse. The strapping sorrel gelding, Colt, was his mountain horse. With the distinctive 2L brand seared into their left hindquarters, he knew they were his horses.

A week before, he had realized two horses were missing. When he rallied the Night Riders, he left the house that night, ready to send a message. With the rustlers surrounded, he instructed the Night Riders to prepare a noose around the neck of each of the four bandits and tie their hands together. While pointing to the fir, he locked eyes with the men. "The large fir tree will serve as the hanging tree, and we'll cut the horses loose once we're ready." The five nodded and carried out the instructions.

After they had the preparations in order, he rode over on his horse and ensured the rustlers kicked their feet out of the stirrups. He motioned to two men to grab the reins to prevent the horses from running off. With everyone in place, Great-Grandpa Lee addressed the group.

"We're gathered here today to send a message that we will not tolerate thievery or other nefarious actions here in the McGrath Valley. Although my brothers and I may face damnation, our efforts to secure a future for our children and great-grandchildren are not in vain. We have caught you in the act of cattle rustling and we enforce the role of judge, jury, and executioner. Do you have anything to say?" His words lingered as an owl hooted from above, foreshadowing the events about to unfold.

The rustlers were silent and avoided eye contact, so Great-Grandpa Lee gave the order. After a slap on their rumps, the horses ran ahead. The four rustlers dangled from the large fir branch. Their bodies jerked and convulsed, and as quickly as it started, it was over. Great-Grandpa Lee mentioned he could see the moment their spirits left their physical bodies.

Despite the brutality, there was a sliver of compassion. Great-Grandpa Lee was exacting and lethal, but not cruel or excessive. "Grab a shovel and show these men some decency," he said as he dismounted his horse, shovel in hand, and headed deeper into the trees. The Night Riders split up. Three men joined him in burying the bodies, while the other two cared for the animals.

The full moon illuminated the valley while spotlighting everything the Night Riders wanted to hide. Four men swung from the large fir tree and the rhythmic sound of shovels clanked in the night. When the owl returned, his hooting pierced the pervasive emptiness, echoing through the canyons and graves below.

"We can let them down now and bring them over to the graves," Great-Grandpa Lee said as he gestured toward the fir. The three Night Riders agreed and walked over. Once they reached the fir tree, a tall man with a red beard untied and lowered the first rope. He repeated the process until they were all on the ground. A distinct smell of tobacco smoke, embedded in clothing, wafted from one rustler. None of the Night Riders uttered a word during the somber ordeal.

One by one, they threw a body over their shoulder. Next, they lowered the bodies into the graves and climbed out. With the last one, the Night Riders stood around the graves in silence. After removing their cowboy hats, they looked at the bodies with rope burns around their necks. Their eyes met a look of pure horror etched onto the rustlers' ashen faces. One of the men shuddered at the sight.

With cowboy hats in hand, the vigilantes said, "Rest in peace." Great-Grandpa Lee put his hat back on and then grabbed his shovel. While glancing at each other, the Night Riders realized this act changed the rest of their lives. They were accessories to murder, and there was no coming back from that. The rest of the men grabbed shovels and joined him.

After they filled in the graves with dirt, they gathered rocks to anchor the crosses made with branches and leather. "Looks like we're done here," Great-Grandpa Lee said. "It's almost midnight. Let's gather the horses, join the herd, stay overnight, and leave early."

When they joined the other Night Riders and the herd, they concluded the evening and removed the saddles and blankets. A tangy and sour smell permeated the area. They unbridled their horses and used their ropes to make a rope halter and lead for each horse. With six riders and twelve ropes, they covered the ten horses. They also had enough rope to make a highline tied between two trees to secure the leads. The ropes they used to make nooses were now haltering horses.

The Night Riders stared at the bright full moon as the heaviness of the day faded into the darkness. "What happened here today doesn't leave this group," Great-Grandpa Lee said, stroking his bushy mustache. While the five other men nodded, thousand-yard stares crept over their faces. "What happens in the McGrath Valley stays in the McGrath Valley."

Despite an eventful evening, Great-Grandpa Lee took watch that night over the horses and cattle. It was a calm night, and the stillness helped quiet his mind. He grabbed his notebook and began writing his thoughts. It was a confession of sorts, though written in Shoshone with key dates, names, and places changed to protect the identities of those involved.

When he finished, he ripped out the page. He held it before he tossed it in the campfire. The words on the page felt profound to him. He learned many years ago that journaling was cathartic to him, and when he burned the pages, he further solidified, releasing these events from his mind.

Even though Great-Grandpa Lee believed hell was his destiny, he refused to endure misery on Earth. So, he embraced journaling and drinking whiskey as coping mechanisms.

The campfire crackled in the night, burning the edges before engulfing the entire page. Within seconds, the flames danced against the dark, erasing the memory of the day. The campfire's trance transported him, evoking nostalgia for his initial journey west.

Although the allure of the West was intoxicating, it was every bit the wild and rugged place he imagined. Nothing could prepare him for the level of brutality that he himself could inflict. Land changes people on an almost instinctual level. The depths to which people can descend remind us we're closer to animals than we care to admit.

Great-Grandpa Lee reflected over a campfire, and by first light, the Night Riders were ready. They took the cattle and horses to the 2L Ranch for sorting. It was the nearest one on the return route, with new sorting pens and a corral. He was proud of the corral and pens, knowing the amount of blood and sweat that went into their construction.

After the Night Riders made their way across the meadow, they entered the steep, rocky canyons. A light breeze rustled the trees as they wound their way through the demanding terrain. The morning was vibrant and beautiful, but they were less than talkative, as the events of the night before had left a lasting impression with unforgettable images. "Lee, excuse my impoliteness, but your calmness last night was almost unsettling," said one of the Night Riders. The man had a pointy black mustache he began chewing on.

Before responding, he pressed his lips together. "I don't like surprises, so I prepare for contingencies. There is nothing more important than ensuring each Night Rider returns to his family," he said. The man who asked nodded, as if satisfied with the answer. The tension lifted from the group and they continued riding, now an hour out from the 2L Ranch.

Upon pondering the observation, Great-Grandpa Lee realized he could never run away from his past. His fearlessness and capability led him far and wide, but his heart remained in Wyoming. The rugged landscapes, pristine mountain air, and abundant wildlife made it the picturesque ideal he envisioned of the West.

Wyoming attracted people in the late 1800s for new beginnings and escape, often both, like Great-Grandpa Lee. His journey was less than a linear one and he covered a lot of country. The Night Riders, along with other settlers, flocked to Wyoming for the Western lifestyle and land prospects. Their love for the area and their way of life created unity and brotherhood. Although he enjoyed the camaraderie of the Night Riders, he kept to himself.

Great-Grandpa Lee, who lived a colorful life before Wyoming, took many skeletons and secrets to the grave, never speaking a word of them. However, on his dying day, he shared one secret with his son, Sig, confirming the Night Riders' suspicions about his mysterious past. Great-Grandpa Lee's love for adventure and risk-taking, which Wyoming symbolized, had shaped his earlier life and led to experiences he kept hidden from others.

Since he left home at thirteen, he grew up fast, leaving behind the friendly fishing villages of New Brunswick, the endless ocean, and the frigid cold. It was adapt or die and he turned his situation around from being easy prey to being a fearless predator. He developed an edge and toughness that defied his tender age. However, Great-Grandpa Lee rationalized his harshness through a commitment to family and making a better life.

Great-Grandpa Lee jerked out of reminiscing about his earlier years when an eagle screeched from above. The sky, a magnificent shade of blue, shone brightly as the weary Night Riders arrived at the 2L Ranch. In the pens, the cattle sorted with ease, as if knowing they would return home. He offered the two remaining horses, a bay gelding and dun mare, to the others, who gladly accepted.

Once they completed the sorting, the remaining five Night Riders divided into two groups to finish driving the cattle, based on their proximity and the number of cattle in each group. The sound of horseshoes clunking across rocks filled the pasture. Hereford cattle kegged up in the pasture, the sun's rays reflecting off their red backs. After they went their separate ways, Great-Grandpa Lee waved goodbye, not knowing when the Night Riders would reconvene next, but he knew one thing: They would be ready.

As the Night Riders faded into the distance, a red-tailed hawk let out a raspy scream. Great-Grandma Lucy sensed her husband's return and headed to the barn. There, she stood in the doorway and waved. At six feet tall, she was a stunning woman. Her jet-black hair was in a loose bun. But her beautiful blue eyes looked heavy with concern. "Lee, are you okay?"

"I'm glad to be back," he said. Great-Grandpa Lee was a slight man with wavy black hair and green eyes. Their eyes met, and they embraced. She must have sensed he didn't care to elaborate and left things alone. Great-Grandma Lucy was perceptive; she missed little. With a deep connection with animals and people, she could notice subtle cues and signs that others might overlook. When he was away, concerns didn't trouble Great-Grandpa Lee. He knew she could take care of herself.

Tragedy had marked her journey along the Oregon Trail, and if she could overcome that, she could do anything. Her fingertips traced the faint scar on her cheek, a reminder of how far she'd come. When she spurned the advances of a man on the Oregon Trail, he slashed her face, so she shot him with her 12-gauge shotgun.

Lucy, a determined woman, made the journey to Wyoming with sheer grit and resourcefulness. When her parents, Henry and Claire Conrad, two brothers, Jacob and John, and she left Kansas for Wyoming in 1883, she was the sole member of her family to make it. Her brothers perished in a raid by bandits and her parents succumbed to cholera.

Despite losing her family, Great-Grandma Lucy befriended a German family, the Richters. They treated her as one of their own on the same wagon train. She was fluent in German, thanks to her mother, Claire, and could translate for them, which proved invaluable. By perfecting the harsh-sounding language marked by glottal stops or abrupt pauses between words, she made a valuable connection. Since their time together on the wagon train, she taught them how to read and write in English. She formed a lifelong bond with the Richters, who ran a successful general store near Telford.

With the support of the Richters, Great-Grandma Lucy could thrive in Wyoming. She adored Wyoming almost as much as Great-Grandpa Lee, whom she met while working at the general store. Well-educated and articulate, she enjoyed reading, and it was no surprise that her most beloved book was poems written by him. They both shared a love of poetry, and hardships brought them closer.

From tragedy, she gained remarkable strength and compassion. However, her kindness was not to be mistaken for weakness. The shiny 12-gauge shotgun hanging in the main house was her beloved gun. Four tally marks represented painful memories from the Oregon Trail. She endured, yet some memories are better left stricken from the mind.

Like his wife and the Richters, Great-Grandpa Lee and the Night Riders helped each other survive and prosper during tough times. Until the early 2000s, all the families of the Night Riders remained in the McGrath Valley. Now, only the LaRaes were left to maintain the legacy and history of the area.

"So, you might have a future in storytelling, Sierra," Luke said, rising to his feet.

"Your narrative transported me to the Night Riders' world."

"Thank you. I disliked keeping this secret from you both all these years."

Silence lingered among the three before Sierra connected

her account of events to the timeline. Her eyes sparkled as she glanced at Luke.

"When did Dad tell you the secret?"

Luke scratched his head. "Three weeks before the accident."

"That's interesting. It was about the same time that Dad shared this secret with me. He had a premonition, knowing something would occur. Now I understand his reasoning."

"Ruth, you've been quiet. Anything you'd like to share with us?"

"Yes, I thought you would never ask."

"Time for another round," Luke said.

Ruth looked at her watch and said, "So, it's already evening, and we need to check on the center pivots after the system updates. Let's continue this conversation in the morning after chores." Luke and Sierra lifted their gaze, and the three walked outside, hopped on their four-wheelers, and each sibling headed to a different pivot.

While the meadow grass swayed in the warm breeze, the center pivots worked in tandem throughout the night. Tower lights became distant lighthouses in the sea of green hay fields. From an app on their phone, they could control the four center pivots, each covering about one hundred and twenty-five acres. They entered their rotation schedule and other details into the app, a significant improvement from the manual methods they used before with wheel lines.

With enough water to accommodate three of the four pivots at once, it became essential to uphold the rotation schedule. Sierra leaned over her four-wheeler toward Luke. "How about Ruth's missing piece of the puzzle?"

Luke shrugged as they waited for Ruth. "The Night Riders are only the beginning, Sierra." The weight of his words hung in the air between them.

His reply was haunting, like seeing Braden Harris's face at the bottom of Lake Louisa. The memory was a story for another time, she decided, as her gaze fixated on the horizon, which was glowing with amber colors.

Ruth returned, and Sierra awoke after dozing off. The trio rode the four-wheelers back home, sensing an eerie change. Soon after they began uncovering their family history, the story became darker, with shady undertones not visible from the outside. They walked back to the house in silence and called it a night; moon rising, crickets singing, creating space to process the day.

FOUR

Dead to Rights

POCKETS OF LOW-LYING fog surrounded the valley, creating an ominous veil shielding the ground below. Dark storm clouds moved across the sky, and the animals stirred as sunrise approached. Twenty cow elk stood in the meadow overlooking the main house, grazing and shaking the rain from their backs.

When the sun emerged over the horizon, a murder of crows joined the elk, cawing and making their presence known. Like a kaleidoscope, the crows' feathers appeared iridescent in the sunlight when they hopped around near a lone coyote. The sunlight glistened on the tree leaves and blades of grass as the fog lifted.

Vibrant golden hues that commanded attention filled the sky. The siblings gazed at the sunrise and the magnificent, rich colors. Luke's eyelids fluttered shut as he drew a deep breath, savoring the invigorating scent of rainfall reviving the landscape. "We're rewarded by sunrises and sunsets," he said while pointing out the sheer beauty of the vista.

"We're lucky in ways that count," Sierra said, glancing over her shoulder.

They walked back to the main house, mesmerized by the serene morning. While savoring the sunrise and the smell of fresh alfalfa, Ruth stopped and addressed Luke and Sierra. "Let's go to town. I'll grab the keys." Sierra and Luke looked at each other with wide eyes.

"So, where are we going, Ruth?"

"It's better if I show you." The three loaded into Ruth's silver Ram 2500 truck and headed for town. It was a bumpy ride with a lot of anticipation. When Sierra broke the silence, they were a few miles from the pavement. "What's in town?"

"A safe deposit box with documents," Ruth said, adjusting her rearview mirror.

"So, what are the documents about?"

"I don't know. I haven't even seen them. Dad mentioned important documents in the safe deposit box that only he and I knew of. He gave me the key and mentioned that I would know when to share them."

"Okay, this could be interesting," Luke said.

The silver Ram truck eased around the corners of the dirt road with dust streaming behind. Once they hit the pavement, Ruth cleared her throat. "There are security cameras in the vault, so we'll take the documents home to review." Sierra and Luke tilted their heads, then looked straight ahead.

They had five minutes before the bank opened and

Ruth parked the truck by the donut shop, along with several patrons. "Why not park by the bank, Ruth?"

"Because I needed to park here," she said. "Are you prepared? We can't turn back from seeing what's inside." Luke and Sierra showed they agreed.

The first customer of the day, Ruth, retrieved items from the safe deposit box alone. She was gone for about ten minutes, but it seemed like ten hours to Luke and Sierra. Ruth returned and jumped into the truck, blue bag in tow.

"Did you sneak a peek?" Ruth shook her head as she got in the truck, handing the bag to Sierra in the back seat. A few seconds later, a late model black Ford Explorer carrying three people pulled into the bank parking lot. A quick scan revealed they had assault rifles and wore black ski masks.

"Get down." Having the presence of mind to respond, Ruth hit the button to conceal her license plate. Then she accessed a secret compartment under the console that held gloves, a CZ Shadow 2 semi-automatic handgun with a red dot sight, two magazines, a syringe, and propofol. "Sierra, there is a .22-250 rifle under the seat. Cover my six."

She estimated the driver's weight to be around 200 lbs. and prepared the syringe with propofol, put on her gloves, and grabbed her gun. "Luke, call 911 and report a robbery in progress." Before they could say a word, Ruth was gone without a sound. She pulled her hoodie over her head and crouched behind the dumpster to assess the situation.

Ruth ducked behind the Ford Explorer, seeing the open windows. With the syringe in hand, she threw a rock at the passenger side mirror. *Ping*! The rock shattered the mirror.

In a flash, Ruth rushed toward the driver. She stabbed

him in the neck and injected the syringe before he even knew what was happening. *Track marks on his arms and sores on his face. Meth*, she thought. His hair was greasy, and he reeked of ammonia. Before she sprinted off, she slashed a tire.

Ruth jumped into the truck and they exited the parking lot right as the police arrived. Luke drove the speed limit to not raise suspicions. Sierra watched from the backseat as police officers apprehended the robbers. "Whoa. That was intense," Ruth said, with sweat dripping off her forehead.

While tapping the steering wheel, Luke glared at her. "Secret compartments with propofol and a sliding license plate cover. What else are you hiding?"

"So, I have a few surprises. Let's return home and resume our normal routine. Changing sprinklers and fixing fence never looked so good."

"What happened back there, Ruth?"

"It's not a big deal," she said, trying to shrug it off.

"Yes, it *is* a big deal. You're shaking," Luke said, gesturing toward her hands.

"I'm okay. Nellie and Don, the tellers, made me think of Mom and Dad."

"This was too risky, Ruth. The goal is that we stay alive. We lost our parents. Let's not lose more family because of a hero complex."

Luke's words stung. Ruth felt her cheeks flushing. Her skin was clammy to the touch, yet she convinced herself that she needed to remain strong. A wave of sadness washed over her as she considered the potential consequences. While staring out the window, Ruth mulled over the encounter and her siblings' reaction. *He's right. I took a lot of risks and jeopardized our family.*

Since they left for town, it had rained a little, which, combined with the precipitation from the evening before, helped with dust abatement. When they pulled into the driveway, Gus greeted them from the porch, wagging his black and white tail. Trixie was nearby, too. After they parked, Ruth grabbed the blue bag and headed into the house. She stored it in the safe until they were ready to dive in.

Within twenty minutes of arriving back at the house, Deputy Dirk Lancaster pulled up in his cruiser. The distinct black and white color scheme made it hard to blend in. "I'll handle it," Ruth said.

"Hi, Ruth. I need to talk to you about something. There was a robbery at the First Cascade Bank." Ruth was quiet. "First off, I'm not here to arrest you. Although I'll have to be creative in addressing the propofol in my report of the driver. Everyone at the bank is okay and the suspects are under arrest. We have them dead to rights thanks to the driver being incapacitated and having a flat tire."

"Can you keep my name out of this, Dirk?"

Dirk's ocean-blue eyes, summer tan, and megawatt smile made him easy to look at. "Don't I always?"

Ruth tucked her auburn hair behind her ear and felt her cheeks turning red. "Thank you. I owe you big time."

"I'll add it to your tab. Take care of yourself, Ruth." Dirk walked toward his truck, then turned like he forgot something. "So, where did you get the propofol?"

"You don't want to know." Dirk studied her for a moment then tipped his hat. Ruth waved as he drove away, and she walked back to the house. Dirk and Ruth had dated in high school and planned to go to college together. After the accident, Ruth drifted away from him. She was hurting and pushed everyone away except Luke and Sierra. While Ruth withdrew, Luke focused on flying and Sierra tapped into her creativity.

Since she had lost her parents, Ruth forever changed the trajectory of her life. "You ever think about getting back together?"

"He's married, Sierra." After saying that, Ruth paused as if imagining a life with Dirk. *Snap out of it, Ruth*, she scolded. *That ship sailed a long time ago with Dirk.*

Luke winked at Ruth. "Minor detail, right?"

"Luke, you don't have room to judge. What about your old girlfriend, Kelsie Nelson?" Despite their parting ways, Luke and Kelsie remained friends.

"No judgment here; he's a good guy. We're not talking about me, Ruth. How about Chase Langmack, Sierra; I don't want you to feel left out."

Sierra froze and was relieved to hear her sister's voice. After she dated Chase Langmack in high school, he became a top roper in the PRCA.

"Yes, Dirk is a wonderful family man. Let's have lunch and ride Cutthroat Creek to check the grass. Luke, could you pick up Sierra and me on the north end?"

"Of course," Luke said, grabbing his keys.

With a plan in place, they went to the barn to saddle their horses while Luke hooked up the trailer. Buck and Lucky danced around the pasture and gave Ruth and Sierra quite the time catching them. Once they caught the horses, they picked out their hooves using a curved metal pick that resembled a dental hygienist scaler tool to remove rocks and debris.

"Start with the saddle blanket, then the saddle."

Ruth cut her off. "I know how to do it."

Sierra's ears turned beet-red. The leather creaked when she tightened the buckles.

"You could make one of those ASMR videos of the process on social media," Ruth said, realizing she snapped at her sister.

"I could do that. Now I have it, Cowboy ASMR. I might make some videos and post them after all," Sierra said with a playful nudge. They chuckled at the idea, knowing that wouldn't ever happen. Meanwhile, Luke positioned the truck and trailer near the barn and then opened the gate. A squeak filled the air as he swung the gate. With Buck and Lucky loaded, they secured their reins and Luke shut the trailer gate.

Luke rounded up Gus for the ride, and the cheerful dog jumped in the truck and licked him. They went up the driveway with Gus panting, then turned onto the main road. "When do you get your cast off, Luke?" Ruth asked.

"Around the twentieth."

"That's less than a week away."

"I'm pretty excited about it."

Luke looked over at the passenger seat and noticed Ruth fidgeting with her hands. She believed the bank robbery earlier was the day's excitement. Except for diving into the contents of the safe deposit box. *It might be nothing,* she pondered.

However, the closer they were to Cutthroat Creek, the

more she couldn't shake the feeling. She suggested flying the area with the drone first. The idea of using aerial reconnaissance brought her relief.

"Okay, sure thing," Luke said, turning his head toward Ruth.

"You've got a feeling again?"

"I can't let it go, Luke."

"I trust your instincts." Since Great-Grandma Lucy, the women in the LaRae family had an incredible intuition that some might call a sixth sense.

"Sierra, what is your read?"

"I'm picking up on some darkness. With each passing mile, the sensation intensifies."

After Ruth shared her hunch, they were on high alert, and the drone would explore Cutthroat Creek first. Once they arrived at the rendezvous point, Luke backed in to make for a quick exit.

Ruth stepped out of the truck and grabbed her backpack with the drone. She hadn't put the drone in her saddlebag as usual. *Something is different today.* After preparing the drone, she took to the air. Luke and Sierra huddled around the remote controller and watched the drone from the display screen.

A familiar nervousness filled the horse's whinny as Gus whimpered. Ruth's heart sank to her stomach, and she became nauseated as the painful memories surged like a flash flood. The last time she felt this way, she lost her horse, fractured her skull, and had three hundred sutures after surviving a grizzly bear attack. Although it was a dark time for Ruth, she never shared how much the ordeal affected her. While focusing on her breathing, she chanted the mantra, "Peace in, pain out," like her Grandma Sally taught her.

✯ ✯ ✯

When Ruth was sixteen, she and her father were riding Cutthroat Creek in late April to check the fences after a snow-filled winter. They split up to cover the ground on that fateful day. With rifles and bear spray, they headed out. Ruth brought her 7mm Remington Magnum with a muzzle brake, a gift she had received for her sixteenth birthday.

She wasn't an hour into the ride when she picked up fresh bear tracks and scat. The hair on her neck bristled. Ace, a beautiful bay gelding she used for roping, tensed up and whinnied. "It's okay, Ace," she said, stroking his neck. But a few minutes later, Ruth heard a growl…then thrashing in the brush.

Before Ruth could grab her rifle from the scabbard, she crashed down the slope. It felt like slow motion as she kicked her feet out of the stirrups. While falling, her horse, crushed her leg. Ace continued tumbling down the slope as she lay unconscious on the ground. When she came to, she could hear bones snapping. A chill went down her spine.

The grizzly, a large boar, was feasting on her horse. Dazed and bloody, Ruth crawled to retrieve her rifle. However, the bone in her left leg protruded from her calf. Any movement caused excruciating pain. She saw her rifle twenty feet away, and the bear locked eyes with her. He stood on his hind legs and sniffed the air. At warp speed, he lunged at her like a freight train. Full of explosive power and fury.

She crawled faster, but the bear closed the distance in seconds. Ruth was within five feet of her gun when the bear swatted her. He launched her into the air. Now she was opposite her rifle. Unamused, the bear clenched her skull between his jaws.

A warm, searing pain flooded her body. She felt her skull being fractured. While smelling the pungent musk of the bear and feeling his hot breath on her neck, she weighed her options. She could play dead and succumb to the beast, or she could fight. Ruth fought for her life. The raging brute dragged her along by her neck. To her surprise, he moved toward the rifle.

Although she faded in and out of consciousness, she made her move an arm's length from her rifle. She attacked his nose and eyes. Ruth got a few good hits in. The bear's teeth grazed her knuckles. After several attempts, she stunned the bear enough for him to loosen his hold. She escaped the death grip.

Ruth grabbed her rifle. *One chance to get it right*, she thought. When she rolled on her back and leaned upright, she disengaged the safety while steadying the rifle.

The massive creature stood on his hind legs again. She aimed for the throat to sever the spinal cord, buying her another shot if needed. *Pow*! The bear dropped. It was a clean kill. Ruth moaned as the surge of adrenaline made her pain subside.

* * *

Paul heard the gunshot and headed toward it with his horse Rascal, a stocky appaloosa gelding about fifteen hands tall, running at full speed. Within fifteen minutes, he arrived at a scene that no parent should ever witness: his oldest daughter ripped to shreds and bleeding with a bear slumped over inches away. His arms shook, and he dropped the reins.

In an instant, he dove out of his saddle to Ruth. Although barely conscious, she asked her dad to check on Ace to see if he had passed. She did not want him to suffer any longer if he was still alive. Paul was assessing her vitals and injuries, and Ruth was insistent, so he checked on Ace. "He's gone, honey."

She lost consciousness. Paul went into overdrive and his training as a volunteer firefighter and licensed EMT kicked in. He grabbed the sat phone and handheld GPS unit from his saddlebag. As he fired up both devices, he pulled a laminated card from his pocket. The card listed medical extraction locations or extract points organized by property.

Paul was a planner, and his level of preparation was exceptional. The extract point was a few minutes from their location and he called 911 from his sat phone. He conveyed Ruth's injuries and the need for an air extraction, and provided the coordinates to dispatch. He stroked Ruth's forehead and bit his lip.

Dispatch relayed, the ship would be airborne in five minutes with an ETA of fifteen minutes. Paul sighed with relief at the update from dispatch, though he didn't want to move Ruth for fear of a spinal cord injury without stabilizing her. She was unconscious and had a weak pulse. Within minutes, Paul could hear the distinct sound of a helicopter rotor. He leaped on his horse and headed down to meet the medics.

Paul and Rascal arrived right when it was landing. He briefed the medics and took them to her location. Despite severe injuries, Ruth clung to life. The medics worked swiftly and had her packaged in a rescue litter without delay. Two flight medics and Paul carried Ruth to the helicopter. The lead medic informed him they were taking her to Willingston.

As he acknowledged the lead medic, he mentally rehearsed his phone list. The grass and small trees whipped violently from the rotor wash as the helicopter departed. Paul called Penny to update her and ask if Grandma Sally could look after Luke and Sierra. Paul's second call was to his oldest sister, Ronnie. He checked to see if his brother-in-law, John, could free up a backhoe to bury Ace and provided Ronnie with the coordinates. The third call he made was to his friend, Larry Minden, a local game warden, to explain the situation.

With the helicopter en route to Willingston, Paul retrieved Ruth's rifle and hiked below to say his goodbyes to Ace. Upon seeing Ace, a tidal wave of emotion washed over him. He had held it together handling the medical scene, though seeing the look of terror frozen in Ace's eyes, the bone sticking out from his front leg, and his neck snapped with huge gaping wounds and deep claw marks ripped Paul's heart out.

Since he raised Ace from a colt, he was fond of him. Paul's kids and his animals were his world. Seeing Ruth and Ace torn to pieces crushed him. While stroking his mane, he paid his respects. He thanked Ace for being a loyal member of their family until the very end. He took off the saddle, saddle blanket, and bridle and prepared these items for transport. His hands dripped in blood as he staggered toward Rascal.

Paul replayed the events and became nauseated.

Ace and Ruth had experienced an indescribable level of violence and sheer ferocity. Since then, the force of nature had gained a new meaning. While Paul was in shock on the ride back to the truck, Rascal appeared to sense his emotional state. With the truck in the distance, Paul petted the horse. He was reassuring the animal as much as himself. Tough and dependable, Rascal never let him down.

When he needed a mountain and big game horse, his friend Jake Running Deer of the Rio River Nation came through in a big way with Rascal. The sassy appaloosa and Paul, a great team, had traveled many miles together. Once at the truck, he loosened the cinches on his saddle and loaded Rascal into the trailer. Paul put Ruth's tack in the back seat, then booked it for the ranch to leave with Penny for Willingston. He noticed the bloodstains on the steering wheel and the smell of blood in the cab, so he rolled down the windows for fresh air.

As Paul turned down the driveway to the ranch, he could see the concerned looks on his family's faces. Penny had the truck ready and was set to go. Sierra tended to Rascal, her hands trembling slightly. Luke's jaw dropped when he pulled the bloody saddle from the back seat. While packing the items into the tack room, Luke took a deep breath, regaining his composure. Grandma Sally was ten minutes away.

Penny told Luke and Sierra about the bear attack. And

they insisted on helping Uncle John bury Ace because it was what Ruth would want. Their parents agreed and John would arrive in forty minutes. Paul received a call from Larry Minden. He asked him to wait for John to arrive with the backhoe, and Larry agreed. With Paul's truck still hooked up to the stock trailer, he and Penny blazed out of the driveway in their white F-150.

✯ ✯ ✯

Not long after Paul and Penny left for Willingston, Uncle John arrived with the backhoe. They greeted their uncle and loaded their rifles. "We'll be back soon, Grandma Sally." After they hugged her, they loaded up into their uncle's truck. The truck doors slammed shut.

"You ready?" said Uncle John.

They nodded and before they realized it, the trailer was backing into the location for an easy offload with the backhoe. When Game Warden Minden drove up in his truck, Uncle John met with him. He was there to file a report. Uncle John loosened the ratchet chain binders and walked the backhoe off the trailer.

With Ace's coordinates on a handheld GPS, Luke led the way. It took about an hour to arrive at the location with the backhoe. Once they were on scene, Larry got to work. They heard him throwing up in the bushes. After about thirty minutes, he came back and reported his preliminary findings.

"It looks like the bear rushed the horse, causing him to lose his balance and fall down the slope. However, the rider was still in the saddle until about mid-slope, when the horse crushed her, and the horse continued tumbling until he landed here. The bear fed on the horse, then pursued Ruth. After a battle, she escaped, grabbed her rifle, and defended herself."

"That sounds about right," Uncle John said, looking at the hillside.

"I found a fresh elk carcass farther up the slope. The bear was protecting his kill. Ruth is as tough as they come, and I'm thinking of her. Luck has nothing to do with her being alive—that has everything to do with her fighting spirit." After gathering up his gear and shaking hands, Larry headed out. Luke, Sierra, and Uncle John decided it was best to bury Ace in his current spot.

While Uncle John dug the grave with the backhoe, Luke and Sierra gathered branches to make a cross and rocks to anchor it. Sierra had the incredible idea of laminating an Ace of Hearts card from a deck to bring along. Although it was rocky digging, he managed. With the grave dug, Sierra and Luke approached for a closer inspection. "Poor Ace. I hope he went fast," Sierra said, her chin quivering as she fought back tears.

The carnage from the gruesome attack was sobering, cutting to the bone. There was blood everywhere and there were signs of a struggle. While paying their respects, they stood in silence, taking in the scene's totality. After a few minutes, they stepped away. Uncle John stepped back into the backhoe, scooped up Ace with the bucket, and pulled him into the grave.

He dug the grave ten feet deep to deter animals from

digging him up. With slow, controlled motions, he filled in the grave with dirt. The bucket skidded across the rocks as clanging sounds echoed throughout the canyon. After Uncle John finished the grave, he parked the backhoe. Luke and Sierra anchored the cross with rocks and completed the memorial with the Ace of Hearts card displayed on the cross.

"Rest in peace, Ace," they said with raw emotion in their voices.

They all gathered and left the bear where he lay. When they headed back to the truck and trailer, it was dusk and Luke and Sierra's silhouettes disappeared into the distance, their rifles swaying in their slings. Once they reached the truck, they helped their uncle secure the backhoe and jumped into the vehicle. "Thanks, Uncle John. We appreciate you dropping everything to help us out."

"You're welcome. That's what family is for."

Like a casino billboard, his Ram 2500 truck and flatbed trailer lit up the night. They eased around the bends of the rugged dirt road with heavy hearts and minds. Dust streamed behind the truck and trailer like jet contrails. Once back at the ranch, Uncle John walked Luke and Sierra to the house. "Call us if you need anything, and keep us updated on Ruth's status," he said. After hugging them, he walked back to his truck.

* * *

The sound of a truck door slammed as the porch door creaked. Grandma Sally welcomed them inside and they watched the news, waiting to hear from their parents.

"They should be in Willington by now," Grandma Sally said. Her calm demeanor was soothing to Luke and Sierra. She had her sketchbook open and began making smooth strokes with a pencil. An artist, Grandma Sally, used art to express herself. Whenever emotions ran high, she grabbed her sketchbook.

Luke raised his head. "Any updates during our time with Uncle John?"

Grandma Sally shook her head, and they sat in silence, replaying the events and how it all could change their family. Twenty minutes later, Penny called with an update. Grandma Sally put her on speakerphone, and she shared: "Ruth is stable, and she will need surgery to repair the open fracture in her leg. Her skull fractures will heal on their own. She has three hundred sutures on her arms and upper back and the medical team says the next twenty-four hours are the most critical."

"Thanks for the update. We're all praying for Ruth."

"Okay, love all of you," Penny said. With a stiff upper lip and a heart of gold, Penny was the anchor that grounded the LaRaes. As a little girl, Penny remembered her mom, Mia, whisking her and her sister, Hannah, into their Jeep Cherokee in the middle of the night. Her mother's boyfriend owed money to the wrong people after racking up a gambling debt. From the stark mesas of northwestern New Mexico, Penny, her mom, and sister moved to Wyoming for a new beginning. They settled in Telford after their Jeep ran out of gas and the kindness of the locals helped Mia get back on her feet. Penny met Paul in grade school, and they became inseparable. They dated in high school and married after graduation. Together, she and Paul created the family Penny never had. While Penny stayed in Wyoming, her mom founded a spiritual retreat center in New Mexico, and her sister moved to California to pursue acting.

Once she hung up the phone, Penny wept before putting a brave face on for her family. She bit her tongue until it bled to stop sobbing, then took a deep breath and returned to her husband. Penny treasured her family above all else, yet the sight of Ruth's mauled body shattered every hope and dream for her daughter's future, one suture at a time.

***

Ruth survived the next twenty-four hours, and the hospital scheduled surgery the following day to repair her open fracture. However, her skull fractures were still okay and did not dislodge or require further attention. Ruth was ashamed to admit it, though she was worried they would shave her head. With her lion's mane intact, she continued to make exceptional progress, and they released her six days after being admitted.

Her boyfriend, Dirk, stayed by her side at the hospital. Dirk's loyalty knew no limits, past or present. At sixteen, her body healed fast, and she was eager to bounce back.

While the physical wounds would heal, the emotional wounds would take time. She lost her horse and almost her life. That day changed her. She persevered, though she felt so many emotions. Grief, anger, and sadness filled her mind. Yet she didn't blame the bear, but herself for not following her intuition. Although she felt they shouldn't go riding that day, she never voiced her concerns. That decision continued to haunt Ruth to this day.

Upon her return from the hospital, her priority was to pay respects to Ace. Her dad took her back to the location, and she faced her fears. While her heart raced, she heard blackbirds trilling in the distance. She took a deep breath. He was like a hawk watching their surroundings. "How are you doing?" He combed his salt and pepper beard with his fingers like he did when he was nervous.

"I'm okay. Although being here brings back memories, I won't let them define me." Relieved to see that Ace's grave was undisturbed, she placed a full deck of cards in the rocks anchoring the cross. Tears streamed down her face. While shaking, she placed her hand on the grave. "I'm sorry this happened, Ace."

Ruth composed herself and then walked the scene of the attack and described it play-by-play with an air of detachment. When she finished recalling the events, her dad was silent. He told her she described the ordeal like it happened to someone else.

"It did; that version of me died with Ace," she said. "Since then, my focus has been on family and living well. I don't blame you for what happened, Dad. It could have happened to anyone." Her dad looked up and held his hand across his chest. The trip was as cathartic for her as it was for him. With emotions running high, Ruth scanned the area and then hiked over to the bear's carcass, which was in a state of full decomposition. The stench was sickening, but she persisted and grabbed a paw. Ruth whittled off a few claws from the bear with her knife. "You killed my horse, so I took your claws," she said, holding up the claws for her dad to see. He walked toward her for a closer look.

The trip was healing and brought closure to Ruth and her dad. Ruth's youth aided her quick recovery, and she moved past the event. She never took the time to grieve or acknowledge her trauma, so the scars served as a reminder of the deeper pain she kept hidden. Although every scar had a story, not every story needed a narrator.

✷ ✷ ✷

While they watched the remote controller, Ruth struggled to keep her balance. Sierra put an arm around her to steady her. After the bear attack, Ruth's intuition was off the charts, as was her ability to sense bears, or "bear-dar" as she liked to call it. "They're here, I can feel it," Ruth said. In seconds, two enormous bears appeared. Ruth hovered the drone and moved closer for a better view.

"Wow. It looks like two large males in battle."

"Or it could be a sow defending her cubs against a rogue boar," Sierra said, squinting at the screen.

Without intruding on the bears, the drone observed the activity from a safe distance. "Can you spin the drone in a circle?"

When Ruth rotated the drone clockwise, two smaller bears appeared in their view.

"Look, there are two cubs." The sow stood her ground while the boar retreated. Despite being injured, the sow waited until she was certain the boar had left. While taking small, deliberate steps, she walked toward her cubs and moved them to a new area.

"I'm glad the boar didn't kill the cubs, so the female would cycle again," Sierra said with a loud sigh.

"That's a lot of action for one day. I'm happy the bear family is still intact. It hasn't even been a full twelve hours, and it feels like we've lived an episode of mom's favorite show *24* with Kiefer Sutherland," Luke said. "Also, in another week or so, there should be enough grass for the cattle."

"I agree. How about we count our blessings and call it a day?"

"Sounds like a plan," Ruth said as the drone hummed from above. Once she landed and prepared it for transport, they loaded back into the truck and headed home.

Luke turned toward Ruth. "Does this place still evoke memories for you?"

"Yes, it does. I refuse to let my life revolve around what happened here. When Dad and I first came back after the incident, I told him the sixteen-year-old version of me died with Ace that day." Ruth's words cut deep, and the siblings sat in silence for the rest of the trip. Luke put his hand on Ruth's shoulder as she petted Gus's silky hair.

When they pulled into their driveway, Gus arose from a nap. Luke backed the trailer in near the barn and gathered feed for the horses while Ruth and Sierra unloaded the trailer. They led Buck and Lucky to their pasture and turned them loose. "Will you put my bridle in the tack room while I feed Trixie?"

"Of course," Ruth said, while adjusting her shirt.

Sierra swooped up Trixie and packed her while she went to get her cat food. "Nothing but the best for you." Ruth and Luke looked on with their eyes twinkling.

"That cat adores her."

Ruth mentioned Sierra's special connection with animals, and that Great-Grandma Lucy would brim with happiness seeing Sierra.

They walked back to the house and called it a night. Before Sierra went upstairs, she turned toward her siblings. "Let's tackle the documents tomorrow?"

"Yes, let's plan on it. I better bring a flask like Luke," Ruth said, pursing her lips.

After a tiring day, they dispersed into the house. Tomorrow would be here soon enough. Seated at the kitchen island, Ruth stared into the horizon. *In the wake of that harrowing attack, I was resolute—family is everything. I cannot let my guard down again.*

FIVE

Go Through the Mill

THE EXCITED YIPPING of coyotes alarmed the siblings before dawn like a death knell. It startled them awake as if lightning had struck them. Half-dressed, they rushed down the stairs. After snatching their guns and making their way outside, Luke met Ruth and Sierra as they exited.

Ruth had her Winchester .22-250 in a sling on her shoulder and made her way out to the pasture. With her Remington .220 Swift, Sierra went to the guesthouse, where she felt a bird fly past her head, letting out a screeching sound. "It's Gus, come quick!"

Gus was bloody, with deep wounds on his abdomen about thirty yards from the guesthouse. His eyes glazed over, and his once white markings were now covered in blood. Luke and Ruth ran toward them, and Sierra knelt and began comforting their beloved family dog. Luke dropped to his knees and clutched him in his arms, turning his white cast a ghastly shade of red. Gus hung on until Luke could say goodbye and then he passed away. Tears streamed down Luke's face as he rocked his lifeless body. "He's gone." Each word he uttered seemed to ring with the same haunting emptiness of a hollow tree.

A cherished companion, Gus loved the LaRaes, and they loved him. He was a gift from their Grandma Sally ten years ago. After recognizing the remarkable healing power of animals, she had chosen him from PAWS of Jacks to support her grandchildren after losing their parents. She believed he was the right one.

Gus needed a home like Ruth, Sierra, and Luke needed to rebuild their family. He helped Luke through many challenges in life, including the death of his parents and recovering from his plane crash. Gus's bond with Luke was special. To go through the mill didn't capture it. His sisters grew concerned, seeing Luke's devastation unfold as he grappled with the loss of his close friend.

While the pain of losing Gus was still fresh, the LaRaes found themselves in a familiar place: finding comfort in staying busy. Rather than allowing themselves time to grieve, they would compartmentalize and push forward instead. This coping strategy arose from necessity, not coldness. For the siblings, living on a Wyoming ranch, death among pets and livestock was an unavoidable reality.

Ruth approached Luke with a rare tenderness. "Where do you think we should bury him?"

"He loved the shade tree, where he could monitor everything," Luke said above a whisper.

"Okay, I'll grab the shovels and meet you back here."

"I'll make his cross," Sierra said, walking toward the shop. After finding a couple of scraps of lumber from her recent woodworking project, Sierra cut the boards to length on the miter saw. Next, she sanded the boards with a belt sander and then applied a coat of white paint and turned on the fan to help speed up the drying process.

After the paint dried, Sierra grabbed some smaller paintbrushes for detail work. With precision, she joined the boards and drew the word "GUS" and the dates "2013-2023" onto the cross. She added artistic touches, including a sketch of Gus, then gave the cross to Ruth and Luke.

With the grave completed, Luke walked back from his truck with Gus's blanket. While kneeling, Luke wrapped him in his favorite blue plaid blanket and placed him in the grave.

Sierra and Ruth remained silent. They knew Luke needed to attend to his beloved companion's burial in his own way. Luke cleared his throat, staring at the blanket. "Gus was my best friend. He overcame losing a leg, and I overcame losing our parents. His presence enriched my life, and I'm a better person because of him."

He looked at his sisters, who both wept as they paid their respects. They took turns filling the grave back in with dirt. Scoop by scoop, heaviness settled in the McGrath Valley, casting darkness on the 2L Ranch. Once they finished shoveling in the dirt, they gathered some rocks to anchor the cross. "Rest in peace," they said in unison.

After cleaning up, they proceeded with chores and irrigation before breakfast. When they were done with breakfast, Ruth asked what projects they wanted to tackle.

Sierra suggested checking on the cattle at Cathedral Canyon. Her siblings agreed, and Luke would be on horseback. Although he was still dealing with the insurance claims for his Super Cub, Luke decided to take the opportunity to attend to some game cameras while in the area. He appreciated getting out and seeing the mountains and smelling the fresh air.

Luke prepared for his return to horseback riding. His horse, Dixie, a spirited dun mare with a white blaze on her face, would welcome the outing. *I hope she doesn't buck me off*, Luke thought. They walked out to the horse pasture with halters in their hands. While approaching Dixie, Luke greeted her and scratched her neck. Unlike yesterday, Buck and Lucky seemed less on edge and were easy to catch.

Dixie gazed at Luke with adoration, resting her head on his chest. The white blaze covered the length of her nose and forked above her eyes, looking even whiter in the sunlight. With a slight smile, Ruth turned toward Luke. "Looks like she missed you."

"I missed her, too," Luke said, leading Dixie back to the barn.

With three horses in tow, the siblings walked into the barn and saddled their horses. "It's been a while since we've done this together," Ruth said, glancing over her shoulder.

"Yes, I'm looking forward to getting outside the truck."

Sierra smirked while standing beside Luke. "You need a hand? You might be a little rusty."

He shook his head and chuckled. Despite a rough start to the morning, the LaRaes attempted to keep the mood light. Trixie appeared, arching her back and meowing, then jumping up on a straw bale to watch the horses. Sierra had grown fond of her. With her sparkling blue eyes, Trixie looked up at Sierra and purred as she rubbed her ears.

"Sierra, will you take Dixie and I'll get the trailer?" She jumped up and grabbed the reins from him.

Luke swung around. Sunlight reflected off the truck and trailer when he backed up to the barn. He opened the trailer gate as Ruth and Sierra brought the horses. Sierra handed Luke the reins, and he led Dixie in last. The trailer thumped while he loaded the horses. Ruth closed the divider gate with Buck and Lucky in the front compartment, and Luke secured Dixie in the back and closed the trailer gate. The three jumped in and the truck doors slammed, as they headed for Cathedral Canyon, all before nine o'clock.

When Luke rounded a large bend before the switchbacks, a cow moose trotted across the road with a newborn calf in tow. Still shaky, the calf was having a hard time keeping up with her. "Look at the calf, it's all legs."

"Will it ever grow into its nose?" Luke said, scratching his head.

"Their long noses enable them to feed underwater by closing their nostrils," Sierra said.

"Interesting. I hadn't given it too much thought before."

Luke drew attention to the cluster of fireweed, with their spiky pink flowers cascading along the bank. "The wildflowers are starting, too," he said, smelling the fresh berry and citrus notes. The clean mountain air and endless blue sky had a way of making time stand still and worries disappear.

Once they arrived at their rendezvous point, Luke backed the trailer in and Ruth and Sierra jumped out. Sierra grabbed a lunch bag she hid under the seat and suggested they eat lunch first. She made three Philly cheesesteak sandwiches. They devoured the delicious meal without so much as a word among them. After they finished inhaling their sandwiches, they unloaded the horses with Dixie first and Buck and Lucky last; the opposite of how they loaded them into the trailer.

They looked around at each other while tightening their cinches, but Luke edged ahead of his sisters in climbing into the saddle. The leather creaked as he positioned himself. With his left boot in the stirrup, he swung his right leg over and held onto the horn with his right hand. Despite having a broken arm, he made it look easy. Luke glanced at his red-tinted cast and put his hand over his heart. He pointed to the sky as he thought about Gus.

With Ruth and Sierra now saddled up, the siblings rode off. They headed toward Alfred Meadows, where they would split up to cover the ground after Ruth flew over the area with her drone. The meadow grass swayed gently in the breeze, and chipmunks chattered noisily as they walked past. Luke volunteered to take the western flank, so he could change the memory cards and batteries from his three game cameras. When they reached Alfred Meadows, Ruth hopped off her horse and grabbed the drone from her saddlebag. She prepared the drone for flight and was airborne in minutes.

The wind picked up as the treetops swayed. Ruth kept a kestrel, a handheld weather station smaller than a cell phone, with her drone to monitor the weather like wind speed and temperature on site. "We're getting gusts of eighteen miles per hour with steady twelve-mile-per-hour winds," she said. The wind had an icy chill to it and Ruth shivered.

"What is your threshold with the drone?"

"For this model, twenty-six, is the max, though I like to keep it less than twenty miles per hour when I'm flying in the timber." Ruth started flying the area west of the stock water tank, zigzagging across the area before going clockwise. "It looks good over here, Luke."

"Okay, I'll head out, thanks."

"Let's meet here at three o'clock." Luke waved with his cowboy hat as he headed out. Ruth landed the drone in the meadow, changed the battery, and took off. "Sierra, I found the large bunch east of the meadow on the next bench."

"I'll begin here and proceed in that direction. Will you cover the swath from north to east before you get cliffed out?"

Ruth acknowledged Sierra and made passes with the drone until satisfied with the ground she covered. She saved one battery for any unexpected situations before setting out on her swath on Buck.

Luke was close to arriving at the first of three game cameras. He was excited to see the footage. It was his initial return to the cameras since the plane crash. With twelve cameras posted across different sites, he used coordinates to retrieve the cameras and track the movement of wild game.

When he stepped out of the saddle, he noticed claw marks on the tree and ran his fingers over them. He felt the grooves in the tree and imagined the force that had made them. *Well, at least the camera is unscathed,* he pondered. He replaced the batteries, followed by the memory card, and repeated the steps for the two other cameras. Pikas squeaked as Luke and Dixie rode by.

After he finished with the game cameras, he continued riding the western flank. "Months of being inactive made me realize how I miss horseback riding. Mountains purify and offer space for reflection and connection with nature. I have missed this, Dixie," he said as he patted her neck and inhaled the clean, clarifying air. *Mountains healed, yet brought unpredictable swings from peaks to valleys*, he thought.

"Grandma Sally used to say that nature was the best teacher," Luke said as he and Dixie weaved through an aspen stand, the leaves rustling in the biting cold breeze. "She reminded me of finding the middle ground. When I feel myself drifting off course, I think of her telling me to find my center. Today has been a roller coaster of emotions, and I needed the reminder to keep it between the lines."

Like Luke, Ruth and Sierra also benefited from the healing power of the mountains and being alone with their thoughts. The ranch felt heavy, but the rugged peaks offered respite. About three hours passed, and they returned to the meadow. The bright glow of the sun and the sweet smell of wildflowers permeated the air. Their heady aroma was as thrilling as their beauty with shades of red, yellow, and pink filling the meadow like one of Grandma Sally's watercolor paintings.

As if they had lifted a burden, the siblings appeared with eyes shining and heads held high. "We needed this today," Ruth said, rolling her shoulders. Sierra and Luke lowered their gaze as they admired the wildflowers. They stopped to water their horses at the stock water tank before returning to their truck and trailer. The rhythmic sound of saddle leather creaking filled the silence. Once back at the truck, they dismounted their horses, loosened the cinches, and loaded the horses in the trailer in the same order as the morning.

Luke hopped into the driver's seat with Ruth riding shotgun and Sierra in the back seat. The ride to the ranch was silent, but a tranquil feeling spread through the truck.

With the windows down, the cab flooded with the fresh mountain air and sunshine. Luke's face looked emotionless despite his cast covered in the blood of his best friend. Ruth and Sierra stared out the window. Although the sharp, stabbing pain subsided to a dull ache, losing Gus still stung.

Sierra grabbed her notebook and began sketching the wildflowers from the meadow. Her pencil made a scratching sound across the page. Smooth strokes and shadows brought the scene to life. Gus became the focal point of her drawing, surrounded by wildflowers. Tears welled up in her eyes as she thought of him.

When they pulled into their driveway, they noticed a white Chevrolet Duramax parked by the main house. "Do you recognize the truck?" Luke said, looking at his sisters.

"Yes, it's Jake Running Deer. He got a new truck."

"Jake is one of Dad's friends from childhood, right? How long did they know each other?"

"That's correct. Dad rescued Jake when he fell through the ice on a snowmobiling trip when they were teenagers, and they remained close friends long after," Ruth said.

Luke positioned the trailer in front of the barn and they unloaded the horses. After unsaddling the horses and putting their halters on, they brushed the sweat off the horses' backs with a curry comb. Next, they led the horses back to their pasture, giving them lots of pets along the way. Perched along the corral, a flock of quail watched and made a quiet chirping sound.

Sierra returned to the barn to grab their feed, and the three soon turned their attention to finding Jake Running Deer. Walking toward the house, they could see a figure sitting on the porch swing. When they approached, Jake jumped up from the swing and headed down the stairs. His cowboy boots clunked as he walked.

"Good seeing you all," Jake said, hugging each sibling. In his late fifties, Jake had deep creases on his forehead and kind eyes. He wore his long black hair in two braids, and his high cheekbones could cut glass. When she embraced him, Sierra detected a slight smell of sweetgrass lingering in his hair.

"It's good to see you, too, Jake."

"I came bearing gifts," Jake said while pointing to his truck. "Look inside." Luke noticed the cracked back window, so he started there. After opening the door, he found an adorable fluffy puppy asleep on a blanket. Luke's eyes watered, as did Ruth's and Sierra's.

"Coyotes killed Gus today. How did you know, Jake?"

"I have my ways of knowing," Jake said. "Her name is Koda, short for Dakota, which means 'friend.' My Australian shepherd, Lulu, is her mother and my neighbor's border collie, Jasper, is her father. She is special and I want you to have her." They all thanked Jake and welcomed him inside.

Ruth looked in the pantry. "Can you stay for dinner?"

Jake nodded in agreement while Luke cradled Koda in his arms as she slept. "We have a lot to catch up on," Ruth said, putting her arm around him.

"Paul, I sure wish you were here, though I know you're watching over us," Jake said in a hushed tone. He never shared his theory with anyone, but he could sense a deeper truth surrounding the car accident, and trusted Paul's ability to reveal it even in death. With misty eyes, he scanned the living room and focused on the moose head mounted above the fireplace.

Even though they were teenagers when their parents died, they weren't ready for the decisions they faced. However, their family and friends—including Jake Running Deer—provided a strong support system. They overcame a lot and learned even more in ten years.

While staring outside the kitchen window, Ruth took comfort in seeing her dad's salt and pepper beard and her mom's long, flowing red hair in the colors of the sky. As the sun set, frogs' croaking filled the background. A mischief of magpies flew over the pasture, chattering before landing on the horses' backs. It was a peaceful ending to an emotional day.

SIX

A Wolf in Sheep's Clothing

SINCE THEIR CLOSE friend, Jake Running Deer, was their guest, the LaRaes prepared their finest rustic gourmet dishes. Luke fixed his legendary bronco hash with fresh herbs from their garden and cornbread while looking after Koda. With enthusiasm, Sierra took on cowboy caviar, a refreshing medley of tomatoes, avocado, onion, black beans, black-eyed peas, sweet corn, jalapeños, and cilantro. The dishes were stunning in appearance and emanated a flavorful aroma. Hot to the touch, the cornbread was fresh out of the oven.

Ruth worked the grill, taking care of the tenderloin steaks and veggie kebobs. In good spirits, everyone gathered around the dining table once the dishes were ready. While expressing her gratitude to Jake, Ruth raised her glass for a toast. With glasses clanking and laughter filling the air, the earlier heaviness lifted.

The amazing sunset and light breeze enhanced the ambience. Once everyone had finished with dinner and cleaning up, they gathered around the porch to enjoy the fresh air. "I must tell you something important," Jake said. As Ruth and Sierra exchanged glances, the mood shifted. "Ruth, be aware that the robbers have ordered a hit on you. My nephew, who is a corrections officer, works at the facility where they're being held. He'll deal with the robbers, but what plans they have in motion remain uncertain."

Ruth took a deep breath and composed herself. "Is the information reliable?" Jake gestured to show affirmation. With a heavy sigh, Ruth pulled at the collar of her shirt like it was choking her. "Okay. Now I'll track down the leak at the police department. Thank you for keeping me informed, and for always looking out for us. We consider you family, Jake."

"While heeding your words, I express my gratitude. Before the accident, I assured your dad of my commitment to look after all of you."

After taking in the threat's totality, they sat in silence and gazed at the stunning sky. While holding Koda, Luke raised his glass. The rest of the group joined in the toast, yet the dense energy lingered as a shooting star fell from the sky.

Ruth turned toward Jake. "Will you stay the night?"

"Yes, if you'll have me."

When they finished fixing up Jake's guestroom on the main level, Ruth and Sierra went to the porch, where Luke and Jake were.

"Even though I am grateful for your hospitality on this wonderful evening, I think I'll turn in for the night after I call my wife. Also, there is a bag of puppy food in the truck."

"Thank you, Jake," Luke and Sierra said and called it a night, too.

From her seat on the porch, Ruth became lost in her thoughts, mesmerized by the twinkling stars above, as Jake tiptoed up the stairs to join her. "Are you okay?"

"I've been in my head a lot."

"Okay. Embrace both darkness and light, but you choose which prevails," Jake said as he steepled his hands. It wasn't long ago that his wife reminded him of this lesson when he was at a crossroads after their son Tristan was arrested. She helped Jake see that not everything is black and white and there are shades of gray.

Like the stars shimmering in the sky, Ruth's blue eyes sparkled. "My Dad loved this lesson and told many versions of it to us."

"I'm grateful that your dad shared this with his children, Ruth, as it has served me well."

The night sky epitomized Jake's statement about embracing the side you're not ready to show the world. Dark and light contrasted, showcasing the vast night sky and exquisite stars, co-existing in harmony.

Jake paused and composed himself. "There are more challenges coming."

While biting her nails, Ruth looked at him. "I knew you would say that."

Jake expressed deep sincerity, offering help.

"Will you call me when things on the inside are complete?"

Jake turned toward her. "Of course. Do you need anything?" She shook her head. "I'm going to turn in. Have a good night."

After he went to sleep, she stayed on the porch and continued stargazing for several more hours. With only the stars as her witness, she found solace in the darkness. Ruth wiped the stray tears from her cheeks and cupped her face in her hand, staring straight ahead.

As she sat alone with her thoughts, she saw another shooting star glide across the sky. The star reminded her that when one thing ends, another begins and so the cycle continues. *I'll be all right.* The gentle breeze stirred the trees surrounding the main house, almost in agreement, as Ruth returned inside the house to get a few hours of sleep before daylight.

✶ ✶ ✶

Before first light, Luke and Sierra were fast at work making buckaroo breakfast burritos, a LaRae family favorite. The aroma of citrus, cilantro, and cumin wafted throughout the house. With Ruth and Jake joining them, they all sat down to eat at the kitchen island, enjoying the burritos and orange juice. "This burrito is excellent; I taste subtle hints of green chili and jalapeño," Jake said, licking his fingers to savor the flavors.

"Thanks, Jake," Luke said. "The green chili is a gift from a friend in New Mexico, and the jalapeños are from our garden."

Luke and Sierra wrapped the leftover burritos in

aluminum foil for meals on the go. Luke set a burrito beside Jake, and he smiled in appreciation.

Since Jake wanted to hit the road, the LaRaes headed out for chores and to check the center pivots. While Ruth walked Jake to his truck, a low-flying hawk screeched, calling attention to the sun rising above the mountains. "Thank you, Jake. I appreciate you making the trip in person, and we love Koda already."

"That thing we talked about last night. It's taken care of already."

Ruth let out an enormous sigh of relief and put her hand on Jake's shoulder. While the LaRaes waved from the front steps, Jake drove down the dirt road with a cloud of dust behind him. Luke held Koda wrapped in a small blanket, her white front paws dangling. As they walked toward the barn, Ruth relayed to her siblings that the robbers were gone.

While doing chores, Luke put Koda in a blue open-face crate secured to the back of a four-wheeler. She slept a lot and seemed unbothered by the sounds and smells of her new home. For her safety and convenience, Luke also ordered an automatic dog door and some toys. With Koda settling into her new home, he wanted to get her used to riding with him.

After feeding the animals, they left for the center pivots with Koda fast asleep. Since the lightning storm, they wanted to ensure the pivots were in working order, confirmed by the app and field verification, and then returned to the house. As they walked through the front door, Ruth's burner phone rang; it was Dirk. "Morning, Dirk."

"Hello, can we meet somewhere?"

"Sure, same spot?"

"Same spot," Dirk said before ending the call.

"So, what was that about?" Luke said, looking at Ruth from the doorway.

"I'm not sure, though Dirk wants to meet."

"I'll go with you," Sierra said, jumping up from her chair.

"Okay, I'm going to review my game camera footage. Also, they moved up the date on getting my cast removed, so I'm going this afternoon."

Ruth and Sierra whistled and clapped their hands.

"Take my truck. There's a 9mm in the console," Luke said as he threw Ruth his keys.

Once they traveled down the dirt road, Ruth noticed storm clouds building in the west. The sky took on a dark blue tint with purple undertones. Sierra described feeling a stickiness in the air. *It's about thunderstorm season*, Ruth thought. When they arrived at the meeting spot, in a pullout hidden by trees before the pavement, Dirk pulled up in his cruiser. Ruth stepped out of Luke's truck and walked over to him. "Hi, what's going on?"

Dirk's forehead had a deep furrow as he approached Ruth and placed his hand on her shoulder. "There is a kill-on-sight order on you, Ruth." She gasped before the color faded from her face. "The robbers, three felons from Colorado, have extensive priors in drug-related crimes ranging from manufacturing to trafficking. Bobby Jones was the driver, while Levi Wright and Eli Brant were in the bank. Since you foiled their big score at the bank, they want revenge. They called in a favor with a cartel kill squad, and the threat is credible, Ruth."

"How did they get my name?"

"The robbers are associates of Deputy John Warren, who I suspect is working with Nate Teague."

Ruth ran through the possibilities, knowing how Teague's crew had multiple charges for game violations and drug smuggling. "That's bad news. Warren gave me up on a silver platter."

"I found a GPS tracker on my personal vehicle, and I have my suspicions that was Warren's doing."

"So, what's your plan?"

"I need proof, Ruth. Do you think you and your siblings could help me catch him in the act?"

"Whatever you need." Within a second of finishing her sentence, Ruth received a text from Luke. She handed her phone to Dirk.

"That's Teague's crew and Deputy Warren loading backpacks. They are working together. Where was this taken?"

"Cathedral Canyon, from Luke's game cameras. And he's still reviewing footage from recent months."

"Does he have any video?"

Ruth confirmed there was video footage. She and Dirk discussed burner phones and the Threema app in more detail before they agreed they needed to head back. They waved and headed off in separate directions. While she and Sierra were driving back to the ranch, the storm clouds towered in the distance.

With one hand on the steering wheel, she handed Sierra her phone. When she looked at the photos, Ruth summarized her conversation with Dirk. "That's some heavy stuff. I better dust off my long gun," Sierra said, with fire raging in her eyes.

Sierra never backed down from anyone and wasn't about to start.

"They might have the cartel in pocket, but they haven't met my family." Sierra let her sister's words sink in as she closed her eyes and Ruth booked it back to the ranch. Deep in thought, Sierra looked out the window. With emotions racing, Ruth watched the sensational sunrise while Sierra was quieter than usual.

When Ruth and Sierra arrived back at the ranch, Luke paced on the porch. "There's more."

She walked up the steps with Sierra, and Luke met them with his tablet. He played a video from his game camera.

"Spectacular land with a lot of potential minus the rabid coyotes. We might need to deal with the coyotes sooner than later."

"So, that's Nate Teague, right?" Ruth asked, studying the clip.

"Who do you think the rabid coyotes are?" Luke said with an exaggerated wink.

"I catch your drift. And I take it that's a bull elk he killed out of season on our land, too?" Luke raised his chin, squared his shoulders, and confirmed her assumptions. Ruth sighed as she sat down on the porch. "All right, get ready. Dirk warned me about the robbers being linked to Deputy John Warren and Nate Teague. Also, the robbers enlisted sicarios to assist in settling the score. They want revenge against me for thwarting their bank robbery. Dirk is going after Warren. He'll need us to back him."

"Holy shit, Ruth. That's nothing to gloss over; the cartel is involved?" Luke's voice boomed as he raised his arms.

Ruth paused. "Yes. We need to stay vigilant because it's a kill-on-sight order."

"That's even worse."

"But we hold the upper hand. We know this area better than anyone else does."

Luke calmed down and ran his hands through his hair. "You're right. I'm worried though."

Ruth's eyes pulsated, which was her telltale stress response. "We'll get through this, but we need to work together. Like I told Sierra, they might have cartel connections, but they haven't met my family." Luke clenched his jaw with a pained expression on his face.

While rubbing her eyes, Ruth discussed security options with Luke and Sierra. Luke agreed to back up incriminating footage from his game cameras on an external hard drive and store it in the downstairs gun safe. They concurred on using the Threema app and burner phones for communicating with Dirk on board, too. Also, they would travel in pairs for town visits and backcountry trips. For added security, they would look for tails and check their vehicles for explosives and tracking devices.

Ruth faced Luke and Sierra. "It sounds like we're dealing with a wolf in sheep's clothing with Warren. Sierra, our intuition will be key in helping to foresee events before they happen. Go with your gut and don't take chances. You two are my world." Her voice cracked as she interlaced her fingers.

"We have your six," Luke said as he put his arm around Ruth.

* * *

As the reality set in about their older sister, Luke and Sierra pulled themselves together to drive to town for his appointment. Ruth stayed home with Koda. While in the truck, they discussed their concern for Ruth and the need to stay strong for her.

When they hit the pavement, and were a few miles out from town, Luke noticed a dark gray Suburban following them with California plates. As they pulled into the medical facility, Luke and Sierra assessed their surroundings before stepping out of the truck. With a derringer inside her shirt pocket and a hunting knife on her calf, Sierra exited the truck first. After a few minutes, Luke got out, and they walked toward the clinic. He went into the clinic while Sierra waited in the reception area. Twenty minutes later, Luke emerged without a cast and tapped the bright red incisions on his pasty, scrawny arm.

They walked back through the parking lot on high alert. Once they arrived at the truck, Sierra crawled underneath to inspect it. Not finding anything, they left the area. Suddenly, the Suburban reappeared after they pulled onto the main road. Before Luke could say anything, Sierra beat him to it. "I'm on it, Luke." Sierra texted Ruth the following message from her burner phone: "Dark gray Suburban following us. Going to Three Steps." Within an instant, Ruth replied she would be ready at Three Steps for the takedown.

Paul had told his children if they weren't in the mountains and needed to ditch a vehicle or body, go to Three Steps. The multiple jurisdictions would bury the case in the desolate stretch of cheatgrass. While recalling her dad's words, Ruth grabbed her Winchester 30-06 bolt action with Leopold scope, a rangefinder, a GPS, and some pre-fragmented bullets. She threw in a logging chain and a large branch to hide their tracks. After putting the key in the ignition, she high-tailed it to Three Steps. Her truck sailed across the washboards, the chassis chattering along.

By speeding on the straight stretches and drifting around the corners, Ruth made it to Three Steps in record time. She hid her vehicle behind the gravel pit used by the county and loaded her rifle with the pre-fragmented bullets. Next, she grabbed the rangefinder and her burner phone before hiking to the top of the gravel pit. Grasshoppers swarmed her as she hiked up. The steady buzzing sound of grasshoppers was almost soothing. Ruth had put her gloves on in the truck and texted Sierra that she was ready. It was mid-afternoon, and the sun broiled her pale skin. With her hair pulled back, sweat dripped off her head like a faucet.

Bang, bang, bang! Ruth heard gunfire. Soon after, she observed a trail of dust about a mile out. After positioning herself, she checked the distance with the rangefinder for her desired shot. The screen read four hundred and twenty yards. Sweat beads pooled on her forehead. Ruth used a tactical technique called box breathing to slow her breathing. While holding each phase for a four-count, she inhaled, held her breath, exhaled, and held her breath again. They were closing in on four hundred and fifty yards. Ruth observed the passenger preparing for another shot from the Suburban window before she steadied her sights on the driver. She fired when she held her breath. The driver went down, and Ruth followed her shot through the scope. She noticed the

Suburban swerving and could see the passenger flailing his arms and trying to grab the steering wheel.

Once she pulled open the bolt, the casing popped out, and another bullet filled its place when she closed it. Ruth watched the passenger through her scope and fired when she had a shot. For a couple of tense moments, she waited for signs of movement. Her phone buzzed with the message, "Clear," from Sierra. The acrid smell of gunpowder wafted nearby. Ruth grabbed her two brass casings, rifle, and rangefinder and headed back to her truck. While at the truck, she put on her hazmat suit. She called Sierra and let her know the plan, then put her phone in airplane mode. Luke and Sierra watched the road while Ruth drove her truck down to their location.

When she arrived, the Suburban was in a ditch. She could hear the engine running. Sierra hopped into Ruth's truck. Ruth sat on the driver of the Suburban, reversed out of the ditch, and drove toward the gravel pit. The driver had a facial scar and sported a neck tattoo of a scorpion. With gold rings on every finger, the passenger was hard to miss. Both were head shots. The Suburban reeked of expensive cologne and cigarettes. *No accelerant necessary*, Ruth mused. Luke blocked the road while Sierra and Ruth continued.

About ten minutes later, they were at Three Steps, a pullout where there were different land jurisdictions: Bureau of Indian Affairs, State, and private land. Ruth used the GPS to position the Suburban in all three areas. This would create a jurisdictional challenge for the landowners and administrators. She parked the Suburban and turned off the ignition. In a rush, Ruth grabbed their wallets, snapped a couple of photos, jumped out, wiped down the vehicle, and placed a rag in the gas tank.

Sierra backed into the gravel pit and connected the logging chain to the bumper and large branch. Ruth waved her on, and she began driving forward, pulling the branch to cover their tracks. When Sierra was fifty feet ahead of the Suburban, Ruth lit the rag with her lighter and left in a hurry. She wore shoe covers with her hazmat suit and sprinted to Sierra and bailed into the cab. Sierra traveled down the road toward Luke. Within minutes, they heard an enormous boom. Thick black smoke billowed from the Suburban. The smoke column was visible for miles across the barren landscape.

While dragging the branch, they caught up to Luke, who then took the lead. Ruth removed her hazmat suit and placed it in a garbage bag while Sierra drove. As they came upon a popular shortcut for fishing, Luke pulled in while Ruth grabbed the logging chain and tucked the mangled branch in the back of her truck; it squeaked as it rubbed against the truck bed. With gloves on, she covered the branch and chain using a tarp from under the seat. They followed him to the cutoff, then turned and headed toward the ranch.

About forty minutes after they were back on the pavement, a stream of emergency vehicles rolled by in the opposite direction with lights flashing and sirens blaring. Jackrabbits scrambled from the sagebrush with all the excitement. Despite the flurry of activity, they kept driving and obeyed the speed limit, yielding to the emergency vehicles.

The sky grew darker with pockets of blue still visible, and lightning illuminated the landscape with sharp, jagged flashes of white light. Thunder shook the truck like a slight earthquake. When they arrived back at the ranch, Sierra parked in the shop. Ruth grabbed the garbage bag and set it aside before removing the tarp, logging chain, and branch.

Sierra took the branch outside to cut it for firewood. With a single pull of the starter cord, she brought the MS 440 Stihl chainsaw to life, and the bored out carburetor produced a steady roar that amplified the sound. Meanwhile, Ruth arrived back at the truck wearing a fresh hazmat suit and holding a caddy containing some spray bottles, Luminol, and a black light to check for traces of blood.

When Luke walked into the shop with Koda in his arms, Ruth closed the blackout curtains and turned off the lights. She sprayed Luminol inside the truck and swept the area with the black light. The first pass revealed a small spatter of blood underneath the jockey box. Ruth moved to the outside doors, handles, and tailgate. Luke watched in amazement at her meticulous level of detail.

A strong smell of chemicals emanated from the truck. Ruth turned the lights on and grabbed another spray bottle to clean the traces of blood. She gestured to Luke to turn off the lights, and she made another pass with the Luminol and black light. Ruth gave a thumbs-up and Luke turned the lights back on. After wiping down the bottles and black light, she merged the cleaning waste in the garbage bag with the hazmat suit. They opened the curtains for light, left the truck in the shop with the windows down, and joined Sierra at the fire pit.

Since Sierra had a fire started, Ruth added the garbage bag. The fire pit was dug deep into the ground to conceal the flames and was free from vegetation in the surrounding area to prevent transmission to receptive fuels. She motioned for Luke and Sierra to move upwind to the porch. "Wow, Ruth, you're full of surprises these days. Seeing you go through your vehicle was like watching an episode of *CSI*."

Ruth slapped her thigh for emphasis. "Dad trained me to be a fixer. I had his organization and logistical planning skills, so he wanted me to be prepared."

Luke mentioned their dad must have watched *Dexter*. Laughter eased the tension as they sat on the porch. Koda was sleeping in Luke's arms as he plopped down in a chair.

Ruth clasped her hands. "So, let's start with your trip to town." Luke and Sierra maintained steady eye contact.

"Luke and I noticed the dark gray Suburban with California plates before we hit the city limits. After arriving at the medical facility, the Suburban was no longer behind us, but upon our return, it reappeared."

"Any damage to your truck? I heard the gunfire when you were closing in on my location."

Luke shook his head as Ruth presented a small plastic bag and pulled out two wallets. She retrieved the California driver's licenses issued to Victor Guzman and Ryan Rios, that were likely fake. No cards, cash, or effects were present. Ruth walked over to the fire pit and tossed the wallets in, along with the driver's licenses. Within seconds, the flames engulfed the items, and she stirred the contents to promote consumption.

Flames danced, reflecting the day's events. While taking a cue from Great-Grandpa Lee, Ruth enacted a campfire confession. "Let's be frank, without judgment, given recent events. I shouldn't have engaged during the bank robbery. I'm sorry for putting both of you at risk because of my ego."

Sierra cleared her throat. "Thanks for saying that, Ruth. We depend on you a lot, though you can bring us into the fold more. I saw you crying last night, and it broke my heart. You're not alone, and we're here for you like you've always been there for us. Also, I like this format, the campfire confession."

"That means a lot, Sierra. I should include you and Luke more often." Sierra signaled approval.

Luke pulled a flask from his shirt pocket. "In the last two days, I've filled this twice," he said, running his fingers over his flask. "In all seriousness, a lot has happened. I couldn't sleep last night, so I watched more of the game camera footage, where I found Nate Teague confessing that he disconnected my fuel line. He also expressed disappointment that I walked away from the crash. It's personal with Nate, and I want to be the one who takes him out."

Ruth nodded in approval. They all reflected on Luke's statement as they watched the fire. Sierra used small branches in the pit and stacked the rest in the shop. The contents burned clean, with only ash remaining. She poured water into the pit and stirred the ash with dirt, using a shovel before checking it with her hand.

"I can't wait to see what tomorrow brings. I'm getting the hang of this Jack Bauer thing," Luke said, referencing Kiefer Sutherland's character in the series *24*. They all laughed as they made their way into the house. But the laughter concealed an uneasiness about what the next twenty-four hours had in store. And like that, Ruth's phone rang, and she saw it was Dirk calling. *It must be important for him to call after nine o'clock*, she thought.

"Hi, can we meet? Same spot?"

"Yes, I'll leave now."

"I'll go with you," Luke said. Sierra smiled before yawning, holding Koda in her arms. Luke and Ruth waved to Sierra and jumped into Luke's truck. With a sheepish grin, Luke turned toward Ruth. "So, I figured we needed to let your truck air out a bit."

With the high beams on, Luke and Ruth buzzed down the dirt road to meet Dirk. Soon after, they arrived to find him waiting. She walked over to him and noticed a seriousness on his face. "The gang war escalated into a riot. The three bank robbers and four others perished."

Ruth raised her fingers to her lips to cover her gaping mouth. "Are all the prison staff accounted for?"

"Yes, they were unharmed."

Dirk leaned against his vehicle. "Also, a Suburban with California plates burned down on Longanecker Road this afternoon. Two individuals were present, but their identification will require dental records. Whoever did this had to know what they were doing by placing the Suburban at the intersection of three different jurisdictions. Now, multiple levels of law enforcement are involved. Sorting it out will require time."

Ruth was quiet, pulling herself together. "Thanks for letting me know."

"One more thing, Ruth. The robbers cooked meth for Nate Teague. I'll keep you posted on the Suburban."

"Nate Teague is the common denominator. Go figure," Ruth said, shaking her head.

Dirk flashed his eyebrows and looked at his watch.

"Were you able to get a burner phone?"

He pulled the phone out of his pocket. Dirk had already installed the Threema app and created an account. Ruth entered their information by initials and returned his phone. When she walked back to the truck, Luke waved him over.

"I'm close to completing my review of the footage from the three cameras and have something important to discuss. I have footage of Deputy Warren telling Nate Teague that he thinks you're on to him."

Dirk's face tensed as he clenched his fists. "Thank you for telling me that, Luke. We'll be in touch." They waved goodbye and the truck doors slammed. Luke and Ruth drove back along the dusty road with moths swarming their headlights.

"So, the robbers cooked meth for Nate Teague, Warren is in Nate's pocket, the robbers were associated with Warren, and Nate sabotaged your plane. Unbelievable."

"It feels like we're getting ready to go to war," Luke said, banging his fist on the steering wheel.

"That's because we are. Good thing we're all good shots and our dad was a prepper."

"I knew watching *Dexter* would pay off," Luke said as he pulled into their driveway. He parked his truck, and they walked toward the house, wind howling in the night. When an owl hooted from the tree above Gus's grave, lightning flashed in the distance, creating fractures in the sky like ice cracking beneath the surface of a frozen lake. The valley amplified the deep rumbling of thunder while they trekked up the steps to the main house. After a long day, they briefed Sierra about Nate Teague's involvement in recent events before calling it a night.

SEVEN

Lock, Stock, and Barrel

LUKE RUSHED DOWN the stairs, clutching his laptop and external hard drive. He stopped at the kitchen island, where Ruth and Sierra were watching the sunrise and monitoring Koda. "Check this out," Luke said while he played a video showing Logan Dagerson, the local shed hunter who went missing in May. Despite a massive search and rescue effort, Logan had vanished without a trace.

Logan crouched near a game camera, which picked up his audio before yelling ensued. Next, he stood in front of the camera with his hands up. Nate Teague and Deputy Warren were in the frame and within moments, Nate walked up to Logan with a handgun. Nate fired two shots to the head, killing Logan execution-style. The sound of the gunshots reverberated. Logan fell while Nate and Warren engaged in a heated argument over the situation. Nate mentioned dumping the body off the dock at Lake Louisa. The video ends with Warren and Nate packing Logan's body toward the lake. "Wow. Have you completed reviewing the footage?" Luke signaled he had.

Sierra stroked her chin. "Should we notify Dirk?"

Ruth pursed her lips and made a smacking sound. "Let's check the safe deposit box items first." She noticed Sierra avoided eye contact. "So, what do you know, Sierra?"

"Logan isn't the only one at the bottom of Lake Louisa."

Ruth's eyes widened. "Will you tell us the story?"

"Yes, after chores and irrigation. I need some time to collect my thoughts."

Ruth acknowledged Sierra as Luke walked over to the liquor cabinet. "I better top off my flask today." An unsettled look swept over his face as he exchanged glances with his sisters.

They walked to the barn, and Sierra was quiet. Trixie could sense her uneasiness and rubbed against her leg. "Hi, Trixie. You know when I'm upset, don't you?" Trixie meowed, and Sierra scooped her up and held her close. Trixie's steady purr sounded like a motor. "Let's make you a house cat, so you can roam as you please. I'm willing to work on training you to use the dog door, too." Trixie looked at Sierra with loving eyes and tapped her face with her paws.

Once Sierra set Trixie down, she continued with her chores. Trixie's silky hair shimmered in the sunlight. Sierra headed out to the horse pasture to check on the water trough and petted the horses as she cruised through the pasture. Next, she grabbed her four-wheeler and headed toward the center pivots to catch up with Luke and Ruth. She sneezed while looking at the horizon. The cottonwood fluff drifted through the air like snowflakes. When Sierra arrived, Luke and Ruth were about to leave. "I'm sorry for dragging today and for being abrupt in the house earlier."

"It's okay. I can tell it's difficult for you to talk about," Ruth said, squinting from the bright sun.

"Let's have pancakes for breakfast and then settle into the discussion."

"Best idea all day, Luke." They revved up their four-wheelers and set off for home.

After they arrived and walked toward the house, Sierra looked at Ruth and Luke. "I want to make Trixie a house cat. I'll train her to use the automatic dog door, so there won't be a litter box, if you're all right with me bringing her into our house?"

"Sure. I also ordered two collars, so we have a spare already."

"Of course, I knew it would happen, Sierra."

"Thank you both for your support. Luke, I can help you install the dog door when it arrives." Luke nodded and put Koda down on her fuzzy blanket before he began preparing the pancakes. While Sierra unloaded the dishwasher, Ruth vacuumed the rugs and turned the robot floor cleaner loose on the hardwood and tile floors.

Together, Ruth and Sierra did a cleaning sweep on the main level. Within forty minutes, they had the house in tip-top shape and Luke had pancakes, French toast, and mimosas ready. "Luke, you spoil us," Ruth said, her hands waving gracefully in the air as if she were conducting an orchestra. "How are you doing minus your cast? I realize it was yesterday, though it seems like it was days ago."

"I'm fine and still adjusting," he said while putting a plate of pancakes on the table. The siblings dished up a bountiful breakfast. Luke raised his glass, announcing a toast. Ruth and Sierra held their glasses and joined in while Koda slept.

Ruth spun around in her chair. "Look who's outside."

"It's Trixie. I planned to wait for the dog door installation before bringing her inside," Sierra said, walking toward the slider. Without a hint of hesitation, Trixie came into the house, smelled Koda, and sauntered around before deciding to lie down near Sierra and lick her paws. *Trixie came inside to comfort me*, Sierra thought, her hands shaking.

When they finished breakfast, they sat back down at the island with Koda and Trixie fast asleep. Luke looked up from his mimosa and focused on Sierra. "Are you up for telling us about Lake Louisa?"

"Yes, I appreciate you giving me a little time to prepare." After taking a sip from her glass, Sierra said, "Remember Braden Harris? He never reported to basic training for a reason: He couldn't."

Luke and Ruth raised their eyebrows while Sierra closed her eyes and composed herself as she recounted that fateful day.

✦ ✦ ✦

Before Braden departed for basic training, he yearned for a horseback ride to Lake Louisa. He was eighteen, and I was sixteen. For the trip, I took Duke, our stocky sorrel gelding, and Annie, our gentle white mare. When we arrived at Lake Louisa, we watered our horses and grabbed lunch by the dock. As we walked down to the dock, I could sense a change in his demeanor. I remember he wore a bright blue backpack that seemed odd. He appeared more on edge, and smelled of ammonia. At first, I assumed it was realizing his military commitment, but I soon found out it was different.

Something was off, so I kept my distance. Braden asked if I would wait for him while he was in the military. I was confused and asked him to explain. His face turned bright red, and he stepped closer to me. Braden told me he was in love with me. While flattered, I informed him I saw him as a friend. When I tried to back away, he lowered his gaze and cracked his knuckles. His movements were violent and forceful.

Braden threw his arms up and then grabbed my shoulders. He pulled me closer and tried to kiss me. I pushed him away and screamed at the top of my lungs for him to stop. He shook me like a rag doll before wrapping his meaty hands around my neck. I kicked him in the groin and ran away. Braden snapped. He chased me like a wild animal.

I grabbed my knife from a holster around my calf. *Wham*! He punched me in the face. For a moment, I saw double. There was no question about his motive: only if I would survive. I steadied myself before I lunged at him with my knife. Without hesitation, I tackled him to the ground. It happened in slow motion. Flying in the air. Stabbing him in the neck. I…I slashed his carotid artery and the arterial spray gushed like a geyser. Blood covered my face and torso.

I tasted iron. With flared nostrils and hateful eyes, Braden sneered. "Sierra," he said, gurgling blood, "You're a spiteful bitch," before departing this world.

My hands were shaking as I clutched the knife. Blood ran down my arms and face. One swipe of a knife ended a friendship and a life. Maybe I missed the signs, and he was evil all along. However, I couldn't let my mind wander. It was me and Braden's body now.

My dad's voice ran through my head, telling me to focus on the three-foot world. My whole body shook as I wrapped my bloody arms around myself like a hug for consolation. The wet clothes clung to my arms, and I felt a sense of dread. I let out a blood-curdling scream until I lost my voice, then regained my composure. *I can't fall apart now.*

As the sun set, the wind picked up, and the branches swayed. I felt dizzy after I grabbed the sat phone. When Dad answered, I told him I killed Braden, I was at Lake Louisa, and I needed help with the body. Dad told me to move the body to the middle of the lake, then use cinder blocks from under the dock to weigh it down. He instructed me to dispose of the body, then take care of the horses and build a fire. Before he ended the call, he mentioned I would find everything I needed, and that he expected he'd arrive by nightfall.

After Dad and I talked, I stowed the sat phone and got to work. With the adrenaline still coursing through my veins, I prepared Braden for the firefighter's carry. It seemed karmic justice; me manhandling Braden to his last resting place.

By doing the carry non-stop, I'd leverage gravity and momentum. Braden was heavy, though no match for the adrenaline in my system, and I made the carry in one pass.

While he floated in shallow water, I retrieved three cinder blocks and cables from under the dock. Scanning the shore, I noticed a raft and pole and I dragged them into the water. With the cinder blocks and Braden aboard the raft, I used the pole to pull myself to the lake's center. The sloshing sound of the waves against the raft helped me focus.

From the center of the lake, I divided his body into thirds by eye. I attached cables to the cinder blocks and wrapped the rest around Braden, leaving a little slack. When I had secured the cinder blocks and cables, I said, "Rest in peace," before rolling Braden overboard.

Bubbles rose to the surface while Braden sunk to the bottom. I dove off the raft. The reality set in when I saw him wrapped in cables like a tourniquet of coils and cinder blocks. His menacing eyes stared back at me as if casting judgment. *I killed a monster, no turning back.*

With my rigging holding, I pulled myself on top of the raft and headed back to the dock. Sweat dripped off my forehead and landed on my rusty-smelling shirt. At the dock, I placed the raft and pole in their original position. Next, I walked back to the horses and grabbed the collapsible bucket from my saddlebag and headed down to the lake. I used the bucket to wash away the blood from the grass. The smell of iron subsided. After multiple trips, the blood-soaked grass was now shiny and green. The…earth absorbed the evidence of violence and brutality to nurture other creatures and systems.

Once I stowed the bucket, I scouted the area for a camping spot. Fifty yards in the distance, I found one. As I grew closer, I noticed there was an underground fire pit marked by a rock ring. I gathered some firewood and found a highline to secure the horses. The firewood crunched while I packed it in my arms. I felt the branches scratching my forearms under my sleeve cuffs. Dad considered everything: lock, stock, and barrel. Upon reaching the horses, I grabbed the ropes to make halters with leads, and then fitted Duke and Annie with them.

As I touched the horses' manes, I looked at my bloody hands. My strong, callused hands had taken a life. With light strokes, my fingertips grazed the horses' necks and hours before, they stabbed Braden. Because I felt my thoughts spiraling, I shifted focus to removing saddles, keeping them nearby.

Leads in hand, I took the horses to water at the lake opposite from the earlier events. After I brought them back, I tied them to the highline using a taut-line hitch knot, and I spotted a headlamp off in the distance. I knew that gait from anywhere; it was Dad on Rascal.

When Dad approached, I noticed the concern in his eyes. He asked how I was holding up and if Braden hurt me. I fought back tears and let him know I was okay. Dad dismounted Rascal, and he was on the ground in seconds. He walked over and gave me a hug. His eyes became dewy as he looked at my face.

After taking Rascal to water, I pulled his saddle and saddle blanket while Dad made a rope halter and lead. We secured him to the highline with Duke and Annie as wolves howled from a nearby ridge. Lake Louisa was iconic, yet the events of that day cast a dark shadow. Despite its beauty, underneath the surface was a tale of horror.

When I composed myself, Dad asked me if I was up to walking him through the events. So, I grabbed my headlamp, set it to the red-light mode, and went over the scene. Next, we recovered the backpack. I hesitated when unzipping it. What I found inside shocked me: it looked like a serial killer's kit. There was rope, duct tape, plastic drop cloth, latex gloves, and a bone saw.

The awkward silence enveloped us, and when Dad looked at me, all the color drained from his face. He told me that Braden was going to kill me. For someone I thought I knew, I didn't know him at all. After seeing the darker side of humanity, it forever changed me. I vowed to live my life with the sole purpose of protecting my family, so no one I loved would ever experience what I did on that day.

My words became visceral after the adrenaline wore off and the pain set in; my face throbbed, yet I felt numb. I was in shock. The world started spinning, and I passed out. I remember waking to Dad splashing cold water on my face. I shivered as Dad handed me a change of clothes, telling me I should burn the old ones.

He mentioned he wanted to keep the backpack and repurpose the items. With my eye swollen shut and a broken jaw, I placed the blood-soaked clothes into the fire, watching the flames flicker. The fire popped and sizzled. I felt relieved watching the fire devour the evidence. All traces of that day went up in flames except my flesh wounds on the surface, anyway. What lay submerged underwater was another story.

With the wolves' haunting cry echoing into the night, we developed a plan. Dad made up a story that Braden never showed, and a bear spooked my horse and I fell off. He insisted on my silence about the events, assuring me I'd know when to inform you. The steady crackling of the fire helped calm my nerves. *People plan sweet sixteen celebrations, not conceal a murder.*

Neither he nor I slept that night. The flames were hypnotizing, swirling and flickering in the most wonderful dance. I got lost in my thoughts. *I killed someone today, not a stranger, someone I called a friend.* That realization still smarts to this day.

At first light, Dad and I did another walk-through, and within twenty minutes, we were on horseback and chasing the sunrise. While riding by the lake, I inquired whether there were additional bodies. After a long pause, he indicated there were more, but didn't provide a number. Amidst the suffocating silence, Dad avowed I would know when to reveal the area's dark secrets. Until then, what happened at Lake Louisa stayed at Lake Louisa.

That explained the meticulous level of detail and planning. Lake Louisa had served the same purpose before. Once the trucks were in sight, Dad leaned over Rascal. He explained that being a LaRae demanded unwavering commitment and asked if I was in. I declared my allegiance, and it shaped my life's path. The sun, high in the sky, warmed my soul by its rays. As the clean mountain air cleared my mind, I realized there were no limits for our family or land.

✷ ✷ ✷

Sierra's words were unsettling. Luke dropped his glass and it shattered on the floor. The sound was sharp like the shards of glass. He swept up the broken pieces and regained his composure. When Sierra returned from grabbing drinks, Luke hugged her. "Dad told us Braden never showed up, and that you went riding, anyway. Your horse spooked and bucked you off. That's all. Ruth and I knew something went down based on the clothing change, but we would not press the issue. We had learned the hard way not to challenge Dad," Luke said, rubbing his forearm.

Sierra poured some Irish whiskey into three tumblers and wiped the tears from her face. "The tears add a touch of salt," she said, trying to cut the tension.

"I'm sorry, Sierra. Hearing your story tears me apart," Luke said while steadying himself against the kitchen island.

Ruth was quiet and put her hand on Sierra's shoulder before she raised a glass. Glasses clanked, whiskey flowed, reality swallowed. Ruth's eyes widened as she turned toward Sierra. "Was there drama at the hospital? I seem to remember something about that."

"Excellent memory, Ruth. After we brought the horses home, Mom and Dad took me to the hospital. The doctor became convinced that someone had abused me. Deep purple bruises on my face didn't help. However, I remained adamant about the story and wrote it down for the doctor, as he requested. After a lot of back and forth, he relented and didn't notify Child Protective Services. Three hours later, I left the hospital. They wired my jaw shut to let it heal for the next six to eight weeks.

"It was summer, and the hardest part of having a broken jaw was how I struggled with communicating. I overlooked something that was effortless for me. When I talked, it sounded like a growl. But journaling and drawing helped me find my voice again." Sierra grabbed a notebook off the chair next to her and shared it with Ruth and Luke. They admired her distinct style, inspired by nature and influenced by Grandma Sally.

While reviewing Sierra's notebook, Luke discovered a sketch of a body submerged in a lake. The eyes from the drawing hooked you like a fish on a lure—terrorizing yet captivating, hinting at a story. "Did you ever field questions about Braden's disappearance? Like from the police?"

"No, and he never joined the military; it was all a lie. His guardian was an uncle who became addicted to prescription pills after a work injury, and he faded from his life. Many people let him down, leaving him alone."

"Jeez, that's a new level of deception," Luke said, grinding his teeth. "It sounds like he had a tough childhood, too." Although he knew his sisters were strong, Sierra's story gave him a newfound respect for their resilience.

Ruth was quiet, which was unlike her. Luke called her out. She cleared her throat and lowered her gaze. "I knew the story didn't add up, and it sickens me to think we welcomed Braden into our home. I'm sorry that happened to you, Sierra, and that I wasn't there for you. It saddens me to think you dealt with everything alone and without support. No more secrets," Ruth said, her voice quivering.

Luke and Sierra held their hands to their hearts as if making a promise.

While they reflected on Sierra's story, they heard a truck in the driveway. Luke stepped outside and recognized Lonnie, their cheerful delivery driver, cruising down the road. After acknowledging Lonnie, he put his gun in his waistband before greeting him. Meanwhile, inside the house, Ruth and Sierra cleared the air between them, while Koda and Trixie awoke from sleep. Koda pawed Trixie, who rolled over, unamused. Ruth mentioned she was going for a walk while Luke and Sierra tackled the dog door.

After gathering tools for the installation, Luke suggested using the mudroom, which seemed the most logical place. Also, the least disruptive. To close off the area, they created a dog run before the kennel because of the wraparound porch. Armed with tools and a set of instructions, they got down to business. Sierra welcomed a distraction: installing the dog door. Although sharing her story was cathartic, she confronted unexpected emotions.

With a long face, Luke approached Sierra. "Now I know why you don't like to go swimming."

Sierra maintained eye contact and gestured to the box. Luke nodded and began removing the contents and laying out the parts.

Once the sawhorses were in place, Luke and Sierra removed the outside mudroom door. They worked efficiently and installed the dog door, kennel, and dog run in no time. After completing the installation, they were ready for a test run. Luke readied the pet collars to activate the door and adjusted the sensors while Sierra gathered treats for training. With ease, Koda passed through the dog door. Trixie hesitated, yet the treats won out. When they returned from putting the tools away, they noticed Ruth, deep in reflection, sitting at the kitchen island.

Luke pulled out a chair by Ruth. "Are you all right?"

"Yes, thanks. I did some strategizing on my walk, and we need to keep the footage. If we turn over the video, we give away Lake Louisa and secrets our family has been harboring. We know of Braden and Logan and then Dad didn't disclose a number. Also, I can't shake a feeling about Nate Teague today."

"Okay. You're saying that giving over the video is opening the door. Like what else could turn up there?" Luke said.

"That's right. The truth will set you free, or in our case, could lead to prison."

As Luke and Sierra considered Ruth's statement, their posture stiffened.

Sierra cleared her throat. "So, what's this about Nate Teague?"

"Nate and Dirk have been on my mind, so something may develop between them." Ruth's burner phone rang. "It's Dirk," she said.

"Here we go," Luke said, shaking his head.

"Nate Teague's crew is tailing him, and he needs our help. He said come armed and bring a long gun to Paxson Summit. Dirk mentioned the mineshaft before he cut out."

"I'll get my long gun," Sierra said. She went to the gun safe and grabbed her favorite gun of all time. A Ruger American Predator 6.5mm Creedmoor bolt-action rifle with a Magpul stock and VG6 GAMMA muzzle brake. With her eyes closed, she inhaled the light scent of Hoppe's No. 9 gun bore cleaner that filled the gunroom. This room was her happy place. Sierra then ascended the stairs with her beloved Predator and magazines in hand. While Luke grabbed their guns and ammo, Ruth developed a plan of attack.

"We're going in blind, so our tactics could change. Sierra, you're set up with the long gun to survey the mineshaft while Luke and I cover the flanks. We'll have our thermal scopes and our thermal binos to refine our assessment before we engage, if it all goes according to plan."

Luke and Sierra nodded in agreement as Ruth handed them bulletproof vests. Once Luke grabbed the keys, they made a jingling sound as he petted Koda and Trixie before closing the front door. "We'll be back soon," he said, his words trailing off, carried by the breeze. An owl swooped by and hooted to announce his presence. "That's right, owl. Tonight, I'll embrace the dark through the light of my scope," Luke said while fastening the buckles on his bulletproof vest. The clicking sound of the buckles brought little relief as tensions ran high.

With the guns and equipment loaded, they left in a trail of dust. Fireflies danced in the night, glowing and bobbing in a mystical pattern. After a gripping confession, Sierra focused on her breathing to center herself and soothe her emotions. She needed to be at her best so she could support a rescue mission, not a recovery. The daylight was fading, and the clock was ticking. *Tick. Tock.*

EIGHT

Ride for the Brand

AN ORANGE GLOW filled the sky at sunset on a sultry summer evening. While the shade spread across the fields, Luke's gray Chevy Duramax parted the sea of dust as it drifted around the corners, rattling over the washboards like a washer on the spin cycle. "We're about forty-five minutes out, Dirk," Ruth said before she lost service. "I heard gunshots in the background. Sierra, what do you think about posting up on the bluff opposite the road?"

"Yes, I agree. There are more options that way," Sierra said, searching her blue backpack. Luke glanced in the rearview mirror before doing a double-take.

"Is that Braden's backpack?"

"I found it while cleaning the tack room. After I washed it in disinfectant, I figured it might as well get some use."

"Does it bring back a lot of memories?"

"Yes, though the only meaning the backpack has is the one I assign it. However, I choose to see it as a souvenir. A salty reminder that I survived a gruesome situation and I can overcome anything."

Luke tapped his fingers on the steering wheel. "That's powerful. I would burn that thing if it were me."

"I have to agree with Luke. Whatever works for you, though."

While Sierra pondered whether keeping the backpack was creepy, Paxson Summit was within sight.

"We're almost there; gear up." Sierra handed Ruth her 30-06 rifle with thermal optics and CZ Shadow 2 handgun. Next, she handed Luke his AR-15 equipped with thermal optics and his darling .38 Special revolver.

"Thanks, Sierra. Are you set?"

Sierra tapped Luke and Ruth on the shoulder. He stopped the truck near the tree cover so she would have a straight shot to the bluff above. "I've got your six," she said, closing the truck door. She glanced at them with the Predator on her shoulder. With a quick nod, Sierra raced through the timber and switchbacks, like an agile mountain goat.

The daylight was fading, so they would park soon and run off thermal optics to guide their way into the mineshaft. Luke backed the truck in on a tank-trapped skid road invisible from the main road. With her thermal binos, Ruth glassed the area and detected a group of heat signatures.

While Luke and Ruth prepared to approach, Sierra dialed in her post from the bluff. The hair on the back of her neck stood up, and she shivered. She calibrated her Predator rifle and prepared for a sniper above the mineshaft. After settling into her position, she began tactical breathing as she scouted the area with her thermal scope. The sniper was above the mineshaft, right where she expected. She locked the target in her scope and waited to execute.

"Over there. I see four people and based on the movement, I'd say three are from Teague's crew. We're looking at six hundred yards out, Luke." They grabbed their guns and ammo as she placed the binos around her neck. With all her senses amplified, especially her hearing, the sound of mice scurrying across the forest floor sounded like a rockslide. The powerful scent of fir trees smothered her as she ventured farther from the truck. "Let's stick together until we get closer and then split up." Luke nodded, and they were off.

They moved fast under the cover of darkness. An owl hooted from above, peering down at the creatures scampering below. While using hand signals, Ruth raised her arm and made a fist to signify holding as she grabbed her binos and started glassing. "I have eyes on the four. They're about seventy-five yards out."

Ruth and Luke steadied their breathing using the box breathing technique and drew their rifles. They approached with stealth precision. "You've got right, I've got left," she said as she disengaged her safety.

"Down!" A bullet whizzed above their heads, followed by another shot. "That's Sierra returning fire, Luke. Let's go!" By sweeping right and left, they worked the perimeter, each taking out a member of Teague's crew while keeping eyes on the person they presumed to be Dirk. He lay curled up on the ground with his hands behind his back. While they made their way to Dirk, another one of Teague's crew grabbed him at gunpoint and ordered him to move, jabbing him in the back with what looked like an assault rifle.

A stocky man with slicked-back hair held Dirk at gunpoint. "Come any closer and I'll blow his head off!"

When Luke and Ruth lowered their rifles, Ruth rolled her head while locking eyes with Dirk. After counting down from five, Dirk fell. *Pow*! Sierra shot the guy right between the eyes, dropping him in an instant. They continued assessing the situation for other members of Teague's crew and moved toward Dirk. Luke covered Ruth as she grabbed Dirk and cut the zip ties from his hands with her knife. Since he was in terrible shape, he wouldn't be able to travel far.

"I'll go back for the truck, Ruth. I'll pick you up at the wide spot before the turnoff for the mineshaft."

She waved him on and braced her left arm around Dirk with her rifle in the sling on her right. With caution, she picked a route to the road, though his condition was deteriorating. A pair of white lights pierced through the trees. She realized they were headlights and moved toward them.

Ruth heard footsteps. Her heart pounded. She put her hand on her rifle. Then she realized it was Luke approaching. She sighed in relief. Luke grabbed Dirk's other arm as he and Ruth continued toward the truck. Dirk collapsed, so Luke carried him the rest of the way and Ruth took point. Once at the truck, they loaded Dirk. Sierra was down within minutes. She wasn't even out of breath, and moved like a cheetah: smooth, fast, and lethal, gliding down the switchbacks.

While fading in and out of consciousness, Dirk kept saying, "Ride for the brand." Dirk's unwavering loyalty to their family and the 2L Ranch was unmatched. Ruth's face flushed as she fought back tears holding his hand. *Nate Teague went too far. First, he targeted Luke, now Dirk,* she thought. Her eyes roamed with untamed ferocity, baring her raw emotions.

Sierra reached over her sister to store the guns. After she secured the guns and ammo, Luke wasted no time in leaving the area. Ruth composed herself and was ready to call Doc Grant when they bounced back into cell service. Doc Grant, a military surgeon, was a close family friend. Despite retiring several years ago, he helped the LaRaes off the books. When Sierra broke her jaw, they took her to the ER because Doc Grant was unavailable. The LaRaes trusted him and appreciated his discretion. "Hi, Doc Grant, sorry to contact you at this hour. It's Ruth LaRae."

"Come on by the shop. I'll be ready."

"Thanks, Doc. We're about thirty minutes out," Ruth said as she ended the call.

Luke cut the tension by changing the subject. He looked at Sierra. "That was one hell of a shot. About eight hundred yards, right?"

"Thanks. It was a hair under one thousand yards."

"Good shooting." Ruth patted her on the shoulder. "You're lethal with that Predator. You also nailed the shot with the guy who held Dirk hostage. Bullseye."

Sierra clicked her tongue on the roof of her mouth and looked out the window, watching the crescent moon in the vast darkness. The cool night air jolted her senses. "Even though I grabbed my brass, we'll need to head back at first light to pick up the bodies and brass casings near the mineshaft."

"Good point, Sierra. Let's plan on you and I coming back for that. There is our destination up ahead," Luke said as he dimmed the headlights. Doc Grant was standing outside the shop and waved as they approached. Ruth got out of the truck and Luke and Sierra helped her pack Dirk into the shop.

"Oh, hell, that's Dirk Lancaster," Doc Grant said as he motioned to the table in the shop. While the three placed Dirk on the table, Doc Grant went to work assessing his injuries. "He's lost a lot of blood, and I see one gunshot wound that missed his left lung by a sliver. They tortured him," he said as he pointed to the burn marks on his nipples. "I understand you must leave, but I still need someone to stay and help me." In silence, they stood around Dirk, grasping the fragility of his situation. The possibility of him not making it was unbearable. Sierra and Luke placed their hands on his shoulders, preparing for the worst. Like they were saying their goodbyes.

"I'll stay," Ruth said. "Are you good with what we discussed earlier?"

Luke bit his cheek. "Yep, we got it. Tomorrow morning, we'll come to pick you up and see how Dirk is doing."

They waved to Ruth and Doc Grant as they loaded into the truck. The pain in Ruth's eyes was palpable. After wiping the blood from her face, Sierra stared straight ahead.

While clenching the steering wheel, Luke sped off into the night toward the ranch.

Sierra looked over at Luke. "We're burning both ends of the candle these days and the lines between dark and light are running together."

"I feel it, too. It's like Dad used to say, intention matters."

"That's true, though we're getting damn good at this killing business."

"Well, I can't argue with that. We've always been overachievers."

They processed the day in silence. The clock struck midnight when they arrived at the main house. Luke and Sierra unloaded the truck and prepared for the next round of violence. An hour later, they were fast asleep. Crickets sang in the background like a lullaby to ease their restless minds.

* * *

To arrive at the mineshaft before daylight, they woke up at three o'clock to finish chores and irrigation. A quick night.

Without delay, Luke reached the center pivots while Sierra fed the animals, using a headlamp to help her see. Despite Sierra leaving food and water, Trixie and Koda went back to sleep as it was too early for them. Luke and Sierra cruised through their chores and irrigation. They were on the road for the mineshaft by four o'clock, with the gear from last night plus Ruth's guns for good measure.

However, it was a somber ride up to Paxson Summit. They agreed to set aside emotions and prioritize the task. When they pulled over to their parking spot, another location hidden from the road, they noticed a few ravens circling above the mineshaft. The ravens marked their destination, and they geared up.

In an instant, they sprang into action, swiftly closing the distance until they were within a hundred yards of the mineshaft. Since it was less than an hour before sunrise, Sierra glassed the area with thermal binos. She picked up some heat signatures and waved Luke over. A pack of wolves feasted on the three men from Teague's crew. There were eleven or twelve wolves. It was disturbing to see the wolves feeding on humans, even viewing through the binos. While composing themselves, they both took a deep breath, then continued on their way.

"I haven't seen that many wolves in a while," Luke said. The way he said it made Sierra take notice, and she thought to ask him about it later. Like a flash of lightning, the severity of the situation struck her. Sierra became still and her eyebrows grew closer. "We messed up, Luke. I know we had one vehicle and Dirk was in dire straits. By not putting the bodies in the mineshaft last night, we introduced an additional food source to the wolves: humans."

Luke took an exaggerated exhale before responding. "I didn't think about it that way, but you're right. Although we can't turn back the clock, we can consider this incident for planning future operations." Sierra nodded, then paused; she discovered a bullet stuck in a tree. She presumed it was from the opposing sniper based on the distance. In her back pocket, she grabbed her Leatherman tool and whittled it out. She rolled the bullet between her fingers before she put it in her pocket with her Leatherman.

Despite Sierra finding the bullet believed to be from the sniper, locating the brass Ruth and Luke fired would be difficult. "I found one," Luke said, picking it up. "Here is the second one." He sounded nonchalant about it, like it was effortless.

Sierra shook her head at Luke's prowess. She patted him on the back, and they continued toward the wolves.

It was twilight now. They could see a cluster of dark gray shapes and hear growling and yipping. When they walked closer, they could see drag marks. The wolves had dragged the bodies twenty yards from the mineshaft. It was a scene of utter carnage. A putrid smell permeated the area. Blood matted down the grass. Their guttural growls and menacing eyes darted like death daggers around the bodies, snuffing the light out of anything they encountered. A lone bald eagle circled, waiting for the wolves to leave.

Parts of organs, limbs, and torsos were strewn about in disarray. With ample food, all the wolves were eating. While examining the scene, the two siblings heard the unforgettable sound of flesh ripping off bones. Three bodies served as food for the wolves, obviously their first meal in a while.

Wolves consumed, on average, nine pounds of food per day. However, they ingested twenty pounds when food was plentiful. One wolf, likely the alpha male, snapped a femur like a toothpick and looked at Luke, daring him to come closer. His eyes were cold and calculating; he was sizing Luke up. "That wolf has your number. I'd watch him."

"Yes, we've met before. I'll tell you about it later."

Sierra could sense Luke didn't want to talk about it. She plugged her nose with her fingers and turned away. "Looks like the wolves have this situation handled."

"Let's pick up the brass and guns around the mineshaft and call it."

Sierra raised her hand and pointed toward the slope. "We

need to find the sniper. I shot at the bench above us near the trees."

"Okay, I'll gather the brass and guns here and catch up with you in case we take a different way back." Sierra waved and headed toward the treeline near the bench. Luke hoped the wolves didn't pack off an arm with a gun attached. Despite the chaos of the scene, the guns were close to the mineshaft. He took off his rifle sling and backpack and began piling the guns and brass casings into the main compartment, ensuring the safeties were engaged on the three handguns and one assault rifle. In minutes, he packed the guns, put on his backpack, slung the rifle, and held the assault rifle, then followed Sierra's route.

Sierra stood in the cover of trees and glassed the area for the sniper. Thermal binos worked day or night, without harming the optics. However, they were quite expensive. "There's the sniper," she said. Still scanning the area for predators, she planned her approach. Luke was close behind, so she waited for him before departing.

Like she was marshalling an aircraft, Sierra guided Luke across the slope. "Let's hug the treeline so we're not exposed." Luke gave her a thumbs-up, and they made their way around.

When they came upon the sniper, Sierra noticed a black fishtail braid and she smelled citrus notes. It surprised her that the sniper was a petite female with manicured nails. Her small, stiff fingers with red nails still clutched the long gun. Sierra pried the gun away, a Tikka T3x TACT A1 with a shattered scope. "She had impeccable taste in guns. As we meant to do with the others, let's pack her back to the mineshaft," Sierra said, looking at Luke.

He acknowledged Sierra while admiring the female sniper and her long gun. With two fierce older sisters, Luke applauded strong women.

Sierra picked up the casings, put them in her pocket, and handed Luke the Tikka long gun and the sniper's backpack. She motioned for Luke to hold her rifle. The sniper was small, and Sierra threw her over her shoulder with ease as her thick braid brushed against her cheek. Luke obliged and then returned her rifle.

"I noticed you shot her through the scope. That's next-level lethal." Sierra fist bumped Luke and led the way toward the mineshaft. Her long, graceful legs navigated the descent as swiftly as a deer. Soon, they were back at the mineshaft. It didn't hurt that the sniper weighed less than a hundred pounds.

"Luke, let's check the backpack." By going through the pack, he found some incredible items, including magazines, thermal binos, a GPS, a compass, documents written in Spanish, and a pill he assumed to be cyanide. Luke transferred the contents to his backpack, thinking some items might come in handy.

Sierra laid the woman flat beside the mineshaft. She folded the sniper's arms across her chest before saying, "Descanse en paz. Rest in peace." Drawn to the artistry of tattoos on her forearms, Sierra knew there was a deeper story, especially with the black and gray Santa Muerte one. Despite condemnation by the Catholic Church, many people of the underworld worshiped Santa Muerte, a skeletal woman, symbolizing death, for protection.

After analyzing her tattoos, they took a moment of

silence. Seconds later, they tossed her into the mineshaft with her backpack. Sierra kept her long gun, though. She and Luke glanced around before departing, hearing the wolves.

The sound of crushing and growling devoured the tranquility before sunrise, one bite at a time. Walking back to the truck, Sierra glanced at Luke. "That was a barbaric scene." He curled his lip and cringed as they went single-file to the truck to skirt the shadows.

While at the truck, Sierra grabbed the tracker and the small hammer she brought from the house. Luke noticed the items and rubbed his chin. "Glad you remembered to bring them."

Sierra suspected location tracking devices on the gear and guns, so she and Luke laid them out. They switched their phones to airplane mode and scanned the handguns. No beeps. Next, they moved on to the assault rifle—still no beeps.

When Luke scanned the Tikka long gun, it beeped. Sierra began inspecting it and channeling where she would put a tracker if it were her.

A lightbulb went off. "Of course, the scope," she said. "Because it's removable." They found a tracker under the damaged scope. "Scan it, Luke. I bet there's another one." The scanner beeped again, so Sierra examined it and paused. "It's in the stock." Luke grabbed a small flashlight from his truck and handed it to her. She shined the light inside the folding stock and found two trackers. Next, she unfolded the pliers of her Leatherman and removed both trackers. "Let's run it again." He swiped the scanner over the Tikka long gun, and it came up clean.

Another scan of the items revealed there weren't any other tracking devices. Luke used a hammer to smash the trackers, then scanned them again to confirm their deactivation. Plastic pieces splintered and pinged off the ground. He moved with speed and precision, helping Sierra pack the weapons and items into the truck. "Great idea about scanning the gear."

"Thanks; it was a hunch." Trackers had utility, though it alarmed Sierra to think who could track her. So, she didn't plan to install trackers on her guns. She had experienced being stalked before, and it ended awfully.

While the sun was on the horizon, they loaded into the truck. Luke yawned before pulling onto the road.

"Want to talk about the wolves?"

After a long silence, Luke gritted his teeth before he spoke. "I left out a few details from my plane crash." He tapped his fist on the console. "I heard grumbling after I regained consciousness. When I opened my eyes and looked outside, I saw a black wolf with his teeth bared growling at me. His menacing yellow eyes were like laser beams. In an instant, I realized the wolves smelled the hundred pounds of beef I was flying into the Agerts' remote camp near Basin Creek. I was sitting in a meat buffet and the wolves began circling the plane.

"My saving grace was Phil Agert seeing the plane go down. He was at Basin Creek, getting things ready. Upon witnessing the plane crash, he rode his snowmobile to the site.

"The crash through the trees busted the right wing while the nose of the airplane lay wedged between two towering fir trees. Although branches shattered the plane's windshield, there were no visible holes discovered. An alpha male wolf saw an opportunity. He jumped up on a downed log near the nose of the plane and peered through the windshield. I will never forget the moment we locked eyes. It was like staring into a life-draining abyss.

"I couldn't look away from the snarling wolf's steely glare. Atop the log, he stood his ground and jumped on the damaged wing. By retracing my flight, I remembered seeing the roof of a cabin, so I couldn't be far from the landing spot.

"In the distance, I could hear the roar of a snowmobile running at full throttle. The sound was getting closer, and then I heard gunshots.

"A sense of relief swept over me, and I attempted to move my mangled arm. Within minutes, the snowmobile was at the crash. It was Phil Agert with a sled in tow. Phil mentioned he didn't know what to expect, so he came prepared. He asked me if I was okay and gestured toward the slope before telling me he killed a couple of wolves.

"Phil suggested leaving the meat, but I stubbornly refused. With Phil doing most of the work, we packed the meat and my belongings onto the sled before making our way to the camp. I straddled him and grimaced in pain as he carved his way through the snow. The steady rev of the engine was soothing, and I fought the urge to fall asleep.

"Back at camp, Phil unloaded the meat into a root cellar, then we climbed back on the snowmobile down the road to his truck. We piled into Phil's blue Chevy Silverado and booked it for town. I faded in and out of consciousness, remembering little until the hospital."

Sierra broke the silence. "Same wolf from the crash and mineshaft, right?"

"Yes, it was the same wolf," Luke said, dangling the keys from the ignition.

"Wow, he's gunning for you."

"It gets better. While at the hospital, Phil suffered a fatal heart attack. If he hadn't helped me, he would still be around." Luke's eyes watered as he stared straight ahead.

"You can't think like that, Luke."

"You're right, but it doesn't make it any easier. That's why it's personal with Nate Teague."

Some time passed before Sierra cleared her throat. "I've been reflecting on a lot of things. What brings me the most joy is simple: family, animals, nature, and art."

"Your words are pure gold. Since the plane crash, I've had time to think about what matters most. I agree, it's not all that complicated when you're being honest. Also, thanks for being in my corner. I don't say that enough."

"Right back at you," Sierra said, patting him on the shoulder.

Luke put on his sunglasses to shield his eyes from the blinding sun before he turned into the driveway of Doc Grant.

When they pulled up to the shop, they opened the truck doors and stepped out. Doc Grant walked over from the house and greeted them.

"Good morning, Doc. How's Dirk?"

"He survived, though he still has a battle ahead. He's been through a lot and he needs to rest. Ruth called his boss to let him know the situation and his wife and kids will be back today from Boston."

"Thanks for the update. Dirk's a fighter. I knew he'd dig deep and draw on his inner fortitude."

Ruth walked out from the shop looking haggard. Her eyes were bloodshot, and she had dark circles under them. "Caitlin and the kids landed in Jacks about an hour ago. She's leaving the kids with Dirk's parents and will head over here afterward."

"Okay, sounds like it's coming together. Here, I brought you a change of clothes, too," Sierra said, handing Ruth a bag. She nodded in appreciation.

Doc Grant explained he could give Ruth a ride back to the ranch after he lined up a nurse to care for Dirk. Soon after, Sierra and Luke got into the truck and returned to the ranch. As he steadied his gaze, Luke focused on the road. They were worried about Dirk and Ruth, too. When they arrived at the ranch, he drove up to the house to unload the truck.

After they unloaded the gear, Luke made lunch. He startled Sierra when he spoke. She had a blank expression on her face.

"What do you think about checking the grass at Cutthroat Creek?" he said a second time.

Flustered, she took a moment before responding. "Yes, we could do that today, knowing we need to move the herd within the next week."

"All right, we have a plan." While Luke hooked up the trailer, Sierra walked to the barn to catch the horses. She grabbed two halters and headed out to the pasture. The sun's rays sliced across the meadow like blades of a windmill, with shorter shadows as the sun rose in the sky.

Although Lucky and Dixie didn't want to leave the meadow, after some coaxing with sugar cubes, they relented. Sierra walked back with two horses toward the barn as Luke backed in the trailer. Luke grabbed Dixie's halter and he and Sierra began saddling their horses. Right when Luke threw his saddle on Dixie, Ruth walked up.

"Howdy, Ruth."

"Where are you two going today?"

"Sierra and I are heading to Cutthroat Creek to check the grass."

"Sounds like a plan. Have room for one more? I need to stay busy. It was a pretty rough ride over with Caitlin."

"Like Dirk's wife, Caitlin? Wasn't Doc Grant supposed to give you a ride?"

"That was my understanding, but she insisted." Ruth took a deep breath.

Sierra studied Ruth's facial expression before clearing her throat. "I'll go catch Buck for you."

"Thank you, Sierra; I appreciate that."

After Sierra finished saddling Lucky, she went to catch her sister's horse. The sunlight danced across Buck's shiny back and a magpie hitched a ride. He wiggled his back, and the magpie flew off. While circling Buck, the magpie let out a scratchy rattle sound as Sierra led him from the pasture and did the handoff with Ruth.

"I'll be right back," Luke said as he rushed over to the house. At the house, he ensured Trixie had food and water and packed some things to go for Koda. Luke also grabbed his camera bag so he could replace batteries and memory cards for three cameras at Cutthroat Creek. "All right, Koda, get ready for your first horseback ride." He picked up Koda and grabbed a vest from the coat rack before he locked up the house.

Ruth finished saddling her horse and she and Sierra secured Buck and Lucky in the front compartment of the trailer, and then Luke loaded Dixie in the back. The trailer gate creaked when Luke moved it. He double-checked the divider and trailer gate before he jumped into the driver's seat, with Koda sitting between him and Sierra. Ruth was trying to grab a quick nap on the ride up and was already asleep. "We'll wait until the ride back to hear about her trip with Caitlin," Luke said in a whisper.

Since the valley was sweltering, the cooler mountain temperatures provided a welcome relief. Luke and Sierra continued in hushed tones while Ruth slept. When they reached Cutthroat Creek and got out of the truck, Luke noticed mountain lion tracks.

Sierra followed the tracks and turned toward Luke. "At least they're heading away." Luke gave her a thumbs-up and opened the trailer gate and swung it open. He led Dixie out, tightened the cinches, and put Koda's food and water in the saddlebag. With Sierra holding Koda, Luke swung his leg over the saddle. The leather made a rubbing sound as Luke climbed in. Next, Sierra handed Koda to Luke, and he zipped her up in his vest.

Ruth stumbled out of the truck and grabbed Buck. "Hello, old friend," she said while leading him from the trailer. She tightened her cinches, and her hip made a popping sound as she mounted her horse. "I'm not that old," she said under her breath. It was eleven o'clock when they left the truck. After the tense conversation with Caitlin, she looked forward to the ride in the mountains.

While Ruth stewed from her morning trip, they rode together in the middle before fanning out. Luke opted to take the east flank and head north, so he could attend to his game cameras. With the north flank, Sierra would work west. Ruth would cover the west flank, including the stock water tanks.

"Let's meet back here by two." Sierra and Ruth tipped their cowboy hats, and they were off. The day in the mountains was picturesque, with crystal blue sky, bright sun, and a light breeze that kept the horseflies at bay. Luke zigzagged as he worked through the timber and arrived at his first camera. When he dismounted Dixie, he grabbed his pouch from his saddlebag and outfitted the camera with new batteries and a memory card. Luke returned to the saddle within minutes.

After repeating the sequence twice more, he wrapped up the game cameras. Luke pondered the memory cards as he observed the grass condition. The mountain air smelled clean and refreshing as he took a deep breath, filling his lungs. As Luke rode toward the north, he could see Sierra cresting a ridge and stayed on his course. "How'd your area look?"

"Good. The cows will do well up here. I rode the upper part and I'll take the lower heading back if you want to work your way toward Ruth."

"Will do. Since I already checked the game cameras."

Once Luke covered the ground, he headed toward Ruth and noticed Buck tied to a tree. As he rode closer, he could see her working on the stock water tank.

"Hey Luke, the tank had some debris in the overflow, so it's back working again." The overflow helped prevent the stock water tank from flooding by rerouting excess water when it reached a certain threshold. Leaves, grass, and other items could clog the overflow, which prevented recirculation from occurring.

"You need a hand?"

"I'm good here. One more area to cover, then I'm done."

"Mind if I join you?" Ruth made a welcoming gesture and was back in the saddle when Luke sneezed.

With the dandelions in full force, so were Luke's allergies. Their fluffy white seeds lofted through the air as he sneezed along. Ruth shook her head as she and Luke checked the last part of her swath. "Are you doing all right?" he asked.

Ruth nodded while tilting her head toward Luke.

"Did Caitlin give you an earful?"

"Of course, she said it was my fault and Dirk would always put me over her."

"Anything else?"

"Caitlin believes his loyalty knows no bounds when it involves the 2L Ranch and the LaRaes, and she's tired of it." Ruth scowled and Luke didn't push the conversation further. So, their ride remained quiet, interrupted only by the bugling of a few cranes. "Look at the cranes." As one of the tallest flying birds, cranes had long sinewy legs and a distinct call.

The cranes flew in a circle, and their raspy bugle was strange, but comforting. After finishing out the swath, Ruth spotted a small herd of bighorn sheep. Luke heard the pounding of their hooves. There were seven ewes with lambs running across the meadow. The herd seemed spooked, yet they didn't see any predators. After watching them for a few moments, she turned her attention to the grass. They both agreed the grass looked sufficient for grazing and planned to move the cattle later in the week.

Ruth turned to Luke, her face gaunt and eyes sunken in. "How'd it go at the mineshaft this morning?"

"We found the brass casings and twelve wolves devouring three bodies like Thanksgiving. The distinct stench of death and decay permeated the area. However, it surprised us to find a female sniper. Yes, a female sniper. We packed her back to the mineshaft and dropped her inside. Graphic scene, Ruth."

She raised her fingers to her lips. Although Ruth didn't let on, the wolves eating the bodies triggered flashbacks of her bear attack. She winced as a chill ran up her spine.

"We prioritized extracting Dirk over disposing of the bodies in the mineshaft and I don't regret that. However, we'll need to consider this possibility for future tactical operations."

"I agree, and thanks for handling things. You and Sierra are clutch performers, and I don't tell you that enough."

"Thanks for saying that." A few minutes passed before they could see Buck and Sierra in the distance.

With two tall blondes in sight, Sierra and Lucky, Ruth felt inspired to make the tall blonde drink with gin, vodka, peach schnapps, orange juice, and peach liqueur. Luke liked the idea and volunteered to make the drinks at home.

While the siblings made their way to the truck, they enjoyed the cooler temperatures and endless sunshine. Luke and Sierra's bronze skin highlighted their straight white teeth.

Despite the sun-kissed glow of her siblings, Ruth remained ruddy-faced. As she tipped her cowboy hat off her forehead, they stopped at the last stock water tank to water their horses and Koda before heading out.

Back at the trailer, they loaded their horses in less than five minutes, like they did that morning. Ruth checked the trailer gates and Luke tapped the side of the truck like a drum roll before he jumped in.

When they pulled onto the main road, Luke glanced at Ruth, who was riding up front holding Koda. She tucked her long auburn braid in her armpit to keep it from flapping in the wind. However, Ruth's appearance hinted at a hellish journey. Her bloodshot eyes and chapped lips were a dead giveaway. It was a tough day as Dirk fought for his life.

Soon, the truck and trailer navigated the switchbacks, sunlight beaming on the cab. Luke moved the visor down as he squinted. The sun descended, weaving through the trees, passing the baton to the moon.

I'm all too ready to pass the baton today, too, Ruth mused.

With intermittent cell service, Sierra received a security alert on her phone. "Looks like we have company at the house. It's Nate Teague."

"That didn't take long," Luke said, cracking his knuckles.

NINE

Post the Pony

AS THEIR VEHICLE rumbled over the dusty road, the open window ushered in the cicadas' buzzing symphony, providing the perfect soundtrack to a toasty summer evening. Ruth bobbed in her seat, half asleep. Koda licked her hand, and she jerked awake.

When they pulled into the driveway, they went to work unloading the horses. The frogs croaked nearby, signifying the close of a long day. After putting away the horses and tack, Luke fed the horses and checked their water. Sierra poured cat food into bowls for the dozen barn cats that managed the rodent population, and she noticed a few new cats.

The cat herd was colorful, ranging from solid white to calico, Siamese, and orange. When the cats heard Sierra's voice, they would flock to her like a catnip plant. It was exhilarating to observe her ability with animals, both large and small. While Sierra dazzled the cats, Luke returned to the house with Koda. He paused when he noticed a knife holding a piece of paper on the doorframe. After unlocking the door, he waited for Ruth and Sierra to catch up.

Without hesitation, Ruth walked up and pulled the knife out to free the note. She read: "It's way beyond personal now. Watch your backs. Signed N.T." The slow burn of escalation with Nate Teague had reached a new level and they were on edge. Luke paced around before clearing his throat. "We won't be safe until Nate's gone. Hell, he almost killed me." His words sounded like a wolf's mournful howl. Luke needed his pack, finding strength and safety in numbers.

Sierra shivered and her face turned pale. "It's like Wes Wood all over again." Wes had stalked Sierra and murdered a man who helped her escape from him. Although he was in prison, his impending release date heightened her suspicions about his motives once on the outside.

The emotional toll of being hunted was indescribable. However, Ruth knew she needed to maintain a level head. "You're right, he won't stop. So, we're going to stop him." In two sentences, Ruth shifted her siblings' mentality from dread to determination. She rallied the wolf pack.

Now with fire in their eyes, Ruth suggested reassessing their entire security system and sweeping the place, including the house, vehicles, and livestock trailer for transmitting devices.

Armed with a plan, they entered the house. Luke fed Trixie and Koda before he grabbed the scanner and brought another one for Sierra. To prevent interference, they turned off the wireless internet and cell phones, unplugged the landline, and powered down Bluetooth devices, smart televisions, and microwaves before scanning. Luke took the outside with Ruth and Sierra starting inside the house. They scanned the vehicles, trailer, barn, and guesthouse and came up clean. Ruth searched the porch on the main house and found a recording device inside the Ring doorbell. She disposed of the device and headed inside with Luke to help Sierra. They coordinated covering the remaining areas and began picking up knickknacks and moving furniture.

After another hour, they had completed scanning. Now it was seven o'clock, and they were hungry. "How about tall blondes and tacos?" Ruth asked.

Luke and Sierra nodded like bobbleheads. "Great. I'll prepare the tacos if one of you wants to make the drinks?" Luke took a bow and headed for the liquor cabinet.

Within seconds, Sierra jumped in to help Ruth with the food prep. The sound of chopping, sizzling, and ice cubes clanking filled the kitchen. The fragrant aromas added a scent profile layered with ingredients, including fresh cilantro, tomatoes, bell peppers, and onions. When they sat down at the table, they held their glasses and toasted. They focused on eating more than conversation, with a night full of anticipation and little food.

"So, Caitlin texted me and let me know Dirk is getting stronger and he's out of the woods now, according to Doc Grant."

"That's a relief to hear. Dirk is tough as hell," Luke said while clasping his hands.

Ruth finished chewing before she spoke. "Let's have a

family meeting tomorrow to discuss the recent events, security system, and moving cattle after chores and breakfast?"

"That sounds like a wonderful plan, Ruth. I need to review the latest footage from the game cameras, and I'll start that tonight." Once they had finished dinner, they cleaned up the kitchen and called it a night. As Ruth walked upstairs, she paused as a rush of emotions flooded in. She remembered her parents sitting around the table, laughter filling the house. Her eyes watered and she pinched herself when she realized Luke and Sierra were following her upstairs. The aroma of fresh tacos and pico de gallo wafted throughout the main level, and she hoped it would drift into their dreams, too.

✸ ✸ ✸

Upstairs, Luke grabbed his laptop and began reviewing the footage from the game cameras. He stumbled upon a video that made him freeze: the alpha male wolf. The ferocious wolf smelled the camera and was snapping and growling; it was terrifying even when viewing from a screen. *He picked up my scent on the camera and Sierra's right. That wolf is after me*, he thought.

Since the game cameras could record video or photo, but not both simultaneously, Luke often designated one camera for each in similar areas. In the last set of photos, he noticed the deer were on guard. He kept examining the footage until a particular photo caught his eye, leaving him perplexed. By enlarging the photo, Luke could confirm that it was someone digging and placing handguns in an ammo can.

When he scrolled through the next batch, he identified the person: it was Nate Teague. "I would recognize that skinny horse's face anywhere. I bet money those weapons are ghost guns without serial numbers that were used in murders," Luke said, pacing his room.

After he composed himself, he finished checking the photos and backed up the assortment of Nate Teague footage to an external hard drive. He could hear Eurasian collared doves cooing when he went downstairs to store the drive in the safe. When he spun the dial to the numbers on the safe, his hands shook. Luke paused, took a deep breath, and then opened the safe.

While making his way upstairs, he considered the convenience of a prepared meal. So, he made buckaroo burritos and stored them in the fridge. It was almost midnight when Luke made it back to his room.

Thoughts raced through his mind, sleep a distant memory. *How could someone hate my family so much? Maybe the answer lies in the safe deposit box? Nate Teague is vengeful, so he must think that the LaRaes wronged either him or his family*, he pondered. Luke seemed satisfied with that answer and fell asleep.

✶ ✶ ✶

Before the first light, the trio stirred from their slumber, awakening in succession: Ruth, Sierra, and finally Luke, each rising as if choreographed by the morning's anticipation. Ruth checked the weather on her phone, which predicted triple-digit temperatures and thunderstorms for the next two days, then cooling down. She considered it a good time to review the security system, check the stock water, and move the cattle after the warm weather spell. Prior to starting chores and irrigation, Luke put out food and water for Koda and Trixie. Ruth and Sierra were at the barn feeding the horses and checking their water. They waved as Luke jumped on a four-wheeler and headed out to the hayfields.

Now it was five o'clock and almost eighty degrees outside as sweat beads pooled on his chin and upper lip. Stickiness filled the air, hinting at something brewing in the distance. At the center pivot, Luke inspected the control panel, which functioned like an operations center that started, stopped, and moved forward and backward. It also regulated water usage and could be temperamental. Looking up at the sky, Luke crossed his fingers and patted the control panel. He finished looking over the center pivots and returned to the house.

As Sierra and Ruth walked up the steps, Koda greeted them at the door, wagging her tail and barking. Ruth helped cook the sweet potato hash while Luke ran the waffle iron, and Sierra prepared the island for a breakfast extravaganza.

They sidled up to the kitchen island and dished up breakfast while watching the glorious sunrise unfold. Like an autumn landscape, the sky was multiple shades of red, orange, and yellow, and it was stunning. They took refuge in the tranquility, knowing it wouldn't last.

After an enjoyable breakfast, Luke and Sierra took care of the dishes and cleaned up while Ruth grabbed some items for their meeting. Soon after gathering around the kitchen island, the siblings settled down in a front-row seat of the sun rising in the sky. They sat in silence for a few minutes before Ruth kicked things off. "It's too hot already for a campfire confession, so let's improvise, and have a kitchen confession. I wanted to connect with you and discuss recent matters. Let's start after the Suburban incident."

Luke gave her a thumbs-up and Sierra composed herself before she spoke up. "The discussions about Lake Louisa brought back a lot of memories for me and some unresolved emotions that I'm working through. Although getting justice for Logan involves tackling Nate Teague first. But knowing Logan, he has a GoPro tucked away on his person somewhere. I also agree with what you brought up earlier, Ruth, that we need to review the contents of the safe deposit box before we formalize any plans."

Ruth bit her lip. "What about Dirk's extraction?"

"Luke and I talked about this, and we agreed to consider transportation and disposal options for future operations. However, we introduced the wolves to an alternative food source. Luke, anything to add?"

"Sierra was rock-solid during the mission and picked up on subtleties that I would have missed, like the Santa Muerte tattoo on the female sniper and sweeping the guns for trackers."

"What else?" Ruth sensed he had more to say.

"The latest ordeal brought up feelings of guilt surrounding my plane crash. Phil died because he helped me. It's time for us to take action against Nate Teague. He won't stop until he's no longer breathing. Last night, I reviewed the game camera footage and found Nate hiding handguns in an ammo can on our property. Post the pony or pay up because karma is cashing in," Luke said.

"We're all processing some unresolved emotions. Excellent work managing the situation at the mineshaft, you two. I agree with your assessment of Nate Teague." Ruth took a drink from her glass. "Although I shared part of this with Luke at Cutthroat Creek, I wanted to include you, Sierra. Caitlin believes Dirk has unwavering loyalty to our family and ranch, and she's over it." Sierra tilted her head, and she and Luke didn't press further.

Luke's phone rang; it was the insurance company. "Excuse me," he said as he walked to another room to take the call. After a few minutes, he returned and shared an update. "Good news. They approved my claim and will cut me a check so I can look for a new airplane."

"That's terrific news, Luke. I'm glad it came together."

With a glimmer of good news from Luke's insurance claim, the three continued their discussion. "Anything else to add before we move on?" It was silent, so Ruth proceeded with the next item of discussion: the security system. "Although Dad designed an excellent security system, including a bunker below the guesthouse, do we need any updates?"

Luke opened his mouth and hesitated before he responded. "He thought of everything, including an off-grid option and separate internet connection from the main house." Sierra slapped her hand on the table for emphasis.

"Okay. Our security system seems adequate, then. Ready to dive into the contents of the safe deposit box?" Luke and Sierra gasped as their posture became rigid like an oak tree. Ruth went downstairs and grabbed the duffel bag she used at the bank. When she returned, Sierra squirmed in her chair. After Ruth opened the duffel bag, she set a stack of 9x12 envelopes on the table, followed by rolled maps and a little red book. She noticed a small envelope on top of the others, titled "READ ME FIRST."

When she opened the small envelope, Ruth admired the beautiful cursive penmanship. The perfect pen strokes were mesmerizing. She read the note aloud. "Dear Ruth, Sierra, and Luke, if you're reading this note, your mother and I are gone and you've shared some revelations with each other. Please withhold judgment when you review these materials and realize that, like our ancestors, I wanted nothing more than to protect our family, land, and animals. These ideals put me in the crosshairs of nefarious types who felt entitled to the 2L Ranch and the LaRae name. In case of my death in a car accident, contact Bob Waite for further information. Review contents in this order: envelopes, maps, and the little red book. This information will help you be successful and continue our family legacy. Your mom and I are proud of you. With love, Dad."

No one made a sound after Ruth read the note. There was silence for a couple of minutes before Luke interrupted the awkwardness. "I have had my suspicions but no proof, and now Pandora's box is wide open. There is no going back now. Isn't Bob Waite in hospice?"

"Yes, he has a terminal cancer diagnosis."

Since visiting Bob was time-sensitive, they agreed to review the remaining contents to check for other items to discuss with him.

The note in the first 9x12 envelope was fitting: "Know

your past to navigate your future." Organized by type, the documents included birth certificates, marriage certificates, death certificates, immigration papers, deeds, titles, and water rights. They reviewed the documents and maintained their order, then returned the papers to their envelope.

Ruth opened the second envelope, and like the first one, there was a handwritten note from Dad, this one titled, "Dark List." Luke tapped his foot on the ground with the cadence of a machine gun. The contents were illustrations of the most effective places for stabbing and bullet placement on a body, with a list of considerations when disposing of a body, too. After examining the documents, they placed them back in the envelope.

In the third envelope, there was yet another personalized note, with the words, "Keeping Score" on it. Inside were several pages identifying individuals and how they had acted against, betrayed, or otherwise committed an injustice against the LaRaes going back to 1883. After reading the pages, it was clear these were not petty grievances, but significant offenses, including theft, fraud, and deceit. Once they had read the contents of the third envelope, they carefully placed the items back, and moved on to the next one.

The fourth envelope, titled "A.K.A. Arthur McCray," piqued their interest. Based on how Great-Grandpa Lee acquired Arthur McCray's place, their dad had done more research. He discovered that Arthur McCray was Landry Boudreaux from Louisiana and a deserter from the Confederate Army during the Civil War. Dad suspected Landry killed his own family and burned their plantation to not leave any loose ends behind.

MOUNTAIN OF SECRETS

When Landry Boudreaux arrived in Wyoming, he befriended Arthur McCray. A few months later, he killed Arthur and assumed his identity. Great-Grandpa Lee believed he battled Arthur McCray over Lucy Conrad, not realizing it was Landry Boudreaux. That explained the wooden cross Ruth found earlier in Cathedral Canyon was also Landry.

"Well, that's a dark and twisted tale," Sierra said as her face puckered.

"Karma for the win."

With the anticipation built up from the previous revelations, the last envelope had one word: "Future." Ruth pulled out the papers and reviewed their dad's notes. He had outlined some recommendations for income-generating assets, expansion efforts, and embracing technology, like using drones and game cameras around the ranch. Their dad also detailed perceived issues or challenges he could see his children facing, and first on the list was Nate Teague. Luke acknowledged his father's accurate predictions while admitting his own fatal oversights. His hands were shaking.

Once she noticed Luke's hands shaking, Ruth asked, "Do we need a break?" They wanted to continue. After finishing the envelopes, they proceeded to the bundle of maps. "Any guesses?"

"I'd say maps of secrets. Buried bodies and potential locations for bodies."

"You're right, Sierra. So, here is a map detailing existing bodies." Ruth mentioned the legend included specifics such as the deceased's name, date of death, and the killer's name, if known, along with Xs and numbers.

They rolled out the map and used books and knickknacks

to anchor the corners. While viewing the map, they noticed twenty Xs, with most attributed to Great-Grandpa Lee.

After studying the map, Ruth began unrolling the bundle. The next one was potential burial sites, with the next two covering mineral rights and mining claims and last, expansion opportunities. Ruth applauded her dad's meticulousness in documenting his thought process to support his children. With her trusty Canon 90D camera and all-purpose Tamron 18-400mm lens, she snapped photos of the maps and legends.

One more item to go: the little red book. The note accompanying the red book advised to call in a favor once and avoid using the same contact twice. With a clear chronology, the book organized favors owed by date and the reason. "That's an impressive little book. Dad, Pentagon contacts? Who knew?"

Once she completed another pass of the contents, Ruth confirmed they had completed their review.

There was a long pause before Luke cleared his throat and spoke with conviction: "Dad gave us the blueprints. Now it's on us to follow through." The vulnerability in his voice was perceptible.

The siblings locked eyes and remained silent.

They took a few moments to ground themselves. Ruth took pictures for easy reference. Next, they packaged up the items and returned them to the duffel bag and stored it back in the safe. "It's now a little after ten o'clock. What do you think about contacting Bob Waite?"

"Yes, let's do that," Luke said.

Ruth called him. Although he sounded frail, he said to stop by the garage. He had something to show them. Bob

Waite had a towing business that his grandson was now running.

Soon, they were heading down the driveway en route to Bob's place in Luke's truck. In about forty minutes, they arrived, and he came out to greet them. With a portable oxygen tank and a side-by-side, he navigated the yard.

"Hello, Bob," Ruth said. "We were going through some items our dad left for us, and he mentioned contacting you about their vehicle accident." Bob's blue eyes twinkled despite the haze from advanced cataracts.

"I've waited ten years for this day. And I hoped I lived long enough, so I could tell you in person," Bob said, wheezing between breaths. He gestured to the back. The three walked toward the back of the yard while Bob opened a garage door. They recognized the vehicle; it was their parents' white Ford F-150. The truck was in rough shape.

He proceeded to raise it using a vehicle lift. With the truck in the air, he pointed to a clean cut on the brake line. Bob explained that someone had severed the line, causing the truck to lose control. The siblings broke eye contact as Sierra trembled.

Ruth's posture slumped as she looked at Bob. "Any idea who did this?"

"Nate Teague on the orders of his old man."

"That's unbelievable. Do you know what started the bad blood between our families?"

"A woman: Your Grandma Sally. Nate's grandfather, Wayne, had been dating Sally, though he was abusive, and she had quite a time getting away from him. He beat her up pretty bad and threatened to kill her if she ever left him. So, your Grandpa Sig made sure he never hurt her again. Wayne vanished after that." Bob began wheezing and needed to sit down.

"That explains a lot of things. The generational grudge started over a rivalry that led to murder. Did Wayne have the last name Teague?"

Despite finding out that Nate Teague murdered her parents, Ruth detached from her emotions. She wanted answers, not feelings.

"Yes, Teague."

Ruth connected the name to the map legend.

"Nate's father, Dell Teague, rustled cattle, and your dad caught him in the act, and worked with the authorities to bring him to trial. Your father's courage got him killed. Dell escaped any consequences and continued terrorizing until a stroke forced him to pass the torch to Nate."

It was silent before Bob began coughing and struggled to catch his breath. "Thank you, Bob. We appreciate you meeting with us and telling us the truth. Thanks for holding onto their truck, so we could see what happened. It cuts like a knife to think Nate killed our parents so Dell could avoid going to trial." Sierra and Luke thanked him as well.

"Anything we can do for you?"

"Can I use the truck for scrap metal and parts?"

"Yes, Bob." He gave them a thumbs-up. Ruth, Luke, and Sierra all took turns hugging Bob and thanking him. They waved, then returned to Luke's truck and set out for the ranch.

"One thing remains: Eliminate Nate Teague," Luke said, gripping the steering wheel. The cab felt like a powder keg of emotions. However, with the bombshell news from Bob

Waite, they looked for ways to ignore and override rather than deal with difficult feelings. Ruth had the perfect coping strategy. "Are you all up for checking the stock water at Cathedral Canyon today?"

"I'll hook up the trailer and you all catch the horses?"

"That works, Luke." They all sat in the cab, stunned by the news of learning their parents didn't die in an accident. Nate Teague killed them. It was a lot to accept, and the trip home was quiet.

✶ ✶ ✶

Back at the barn, Ruth stopped to watch the horses and noticed Buck limping. "Would you grab another halter for me, Sierra? I'll take Remy today."

Sierra acknowledged, and Ruth looked Buck over to check his legs for heat and soreness. He was a little tender on the sole of his right foreleg. "It might be a stone bruise," she said to Sierra. Ruth pursed her lips, stroking Buck's mane while walking him back to the pasture.

After Ruth returned to the barn, Luke arrived with the trailer. "Buck's not going today?"

"No, he's limping," she said while approaching Sierra, who had prepared their tack.

"Thanks, Sierra," Luke said as he patted her on the shoulder.

Ruth walked over to Remy, their newest horse. He was a striking black gelding about fifteen hands tall with a black mane and tail, and a white blaze on his face. Remy was a smooth-riding horse and excellent to rope off. Last fall, Jake Running Deer had connected the LaRaes with a woman selling him in Jacks. She and the horse didn't get along, so it wasn't a good match. Luke, Sierra, and Ruth all got along well with Remy, a spirited and dependable horse. Since Buck and Lucky approached their mid-teens in age, the LaRaes had been adding horses to their herd.

Within a few minutes, they had the horses saddled. Sierra and Ruth loaded Lucky and Remy into the front compartment, and Dixie had the back compartment to herself as usual. Luke dashed to the house, promising a quick return. Within a few minutes, he walked out, packing Koda and a bag. "I brought lunch and Koda."

"All right, thank you." Luke handed out buckaroo burritos and lemonade.

"When did you make these?"

"I thought it would be nice to have lunch today, so I made them late last evening. How about some cold lemonade on a hot summer day? It's ninety-eight degrees right now," Luke said.

Despite the near triple-digit temperatures and more family revelations, they looked forward to a peaceful escape as they headed toward Cathedral Canyon. The sun was at the highest point in the sky and cumulonimbus clouds were building near Paxson Summit. "It's hot as all get-out, y'all," Sierra said with sweat dripping from her forehead.

Luke had a big grin as sweat poured off his face and Koda panted. "It's a good thing I threw in some electrolytes," Ruth said above a whisper.

Although sweating didn't purify on a physiological level,

the psychological benefits were obvious. "I think we hit the trifecta: blood, sweat, and tears," Sierra said as the truck and trailer rattled over the washboards.

TEN

Ace-High

WHILE MAKING THEIR way up the climb to Cathedral Canyon, the temperature dropped by almost ten degrees. Cooler temperatures were refreshing, like ice cream on a summer day. The intense heat in the valley, combined with the wind, parched every plant, animal, and structure to bone-dry conditions. "Stay up there, bear. It's way cooler." Luke and Ruth chuckled at Sierra while enjoying the fresh mountain air. Koda was alert, watching the black bear on the bank and growling in a low tone.

"Easy, Koda. When Jake Running Deer said Koda was special, what do you think he meant?"

"I'm not sure, Luke. I guess we'll find out as she grows up."

"Koda can pick up on apex predators, including predatory humans. She may have other talents that develop, too."

"I hadn't noticed that, but I think you're on to something," Luke said while looking at Sierra in the rearview mirror.

They arrived at Cathedral Canyon, and Luke backed in the trailer. When they got out, Sierra looped Luke and Ruth in on her plans. "I sensed Nate Teague would try something today, so I brought my long gun. That's why Koda growled and the bear was running from the area. I'll take a cruise south of here and find a vantage point. My guess is you'll find holes in the stock water tanks and he'll try to mess with the truck and trailer. Ruth, let's send up the drone for recon. I added the suppressor today for stealth mode. When I find him, I'll wing him, though I'll leave the honors to you, Luke."

Ruth rubbed her neck. "I think you're right, Sierra. Nate is planning something today."

"I'll be monitoring my sat phone and these might come in handy," she said, handing the plugs, drill, and hammer to Ruth.

With a plan in place, they unloaded their horses and then grabbed the supplies and equipment. Once they tightened their cinches and checked their sat phones, they parted ways. Sierra placed her Predator long gun in the scabbard, then slipped her foot into the stirrup and pulled herself up. She caught a faint whiff of Hoppe's gun cleaner from the scabbard.

While Ruth and Luke rode together using the trees for cover, Sierra went in the opposite direction, adopting the same strategy. "If I were Nate Teague, where would I be?" Sierra said above a whisper. Lucky whinnied and shook his head. "All right, boy, thanks for the confirmation." Nestled deep within the cover of trees, she and Lucky climbed to a bench with a good view of the surrounding area and several rocks to post up.

Sierra noticed it was quiet, an eerie quiet without birds chirping, chipmunks chattering, or any sounds aside from a slight breeze. She felt Nate's presence as her neck hair stood up. After dismounting, she walked Lucky below the bench to shelter his location from stray bullets. She secured his reins, grabbed her binos, sat phone, and long gun, then made her way back up the bluff. When she returned to her post, Sierra began glassing the area, looking for movement. She stalked her prey.

Near the creek bottom and close to the truck and trailer, she detected movement. Sierra dialed in her Predator. Her scope's rangefinder estimated him at eight hundred yards. She steadied her breathing and waited for him to leave the trees. Nate stepped away from the trees and then paused, like he knew he was being watched. She could see the cords in his neck as he raised his binos. Nate looked like a scarecrow in camo and face paint. He made her location. True to form, Nate puffed out his chest and flipped her off before sprinting toward the trees. With a clear shot at six hundred yards, she pulled the trigger when he was running away. *Pew*! The suppressor muffled the sound. She hit Nate on the back of the knee. *Wham*! He went down, wincing in pain.

While Nate squirmed, Sierra grabbed the sat phone and called Luke. With a steady cadence, she instructed him to go to the truck and mentioned that she had injured Nate. Luke informed her that Ruth would finish her flight and then meet them. He handed Koda to Ruth and gave Dixie her head. She ran fast and smooth like a gazelle across a savannah. Sierra watched Nate through her scope while Luke and Dixie rushed over to the truck.

Within ten minutes, Luke arrived on the scene. Dixie was hot and puffing like a chimney. Sierra called and let him know she was en route. Nate was trying to crawl away when Luke bound his hands with his rope, then put a gag in his mouth and reinforced it with duct tape. Luke began dragging Nate into the trailer and tied him to the divider gate. Minutes later, Sierra joined Luke. "What's your plan?"

"I'm still putting that together…" His voice trailed off as Ruth arrived.

"Would you like some help?" He nodded and Sierra looked at Ruth, then Luke. She explained she had studied the maps of the current and proposed locations for bodies, and there were two potential sites close by. Sierra recommended the closer one, so they could transport Nate using the trailer. Also, she prepared a list of questions for him.

"Good work, Sierra. Do you two have this handled?" Luke and Sierra maintained eye contact and signaled they had the situation under control.

The siblings agreed to meet back at the meadow in a few hours. While Sierra grabbed supplies from her saddlebag, Luke stored her long gun in the truck. He and Sierra loaded up and Ruth made rope halters for Dixie and Lucky. She loosened their cinches and threw her leg over the saddle on Remy with Koda in the seat. Ruth led the horses to the stock water tanks, where she could assess possible repairs.

"We're heading to the old loading chute. It's not far," Sierra said, wiping sweat from her face.

"Got it. I know the way now." The truck and trailer

bounced down the rocky road. In less than ten minutes, they arrived at the location. Sierra put her 1903 Colt .32 semi-automatic pistol inside the waistband of her pants and Luke did the same with his .357 revolver. The Colt .32 was a favorite among pilots, and her Grandpa Sig had gifted her the gun after she won her first shooting competition. Flashes of the past trickled in as Sierra recalled shooting for skill rather than shooting to kill. *I was so innocent back then*, she reminisced as her leather gloves crinkled.

Once Luke opened the trailer door, Sierra piped up. "Let's untie him and remove the gag from his mouth so we can have a civilized conversation." Luke's eyes bulged, though he trusted Sierra's instincts and went along with it. Nate blinked in rapid fire, but he welcomed being untied from the divider gate. Atop the loading chute, a great horned owl with huge yellow eyes stared back at them. He watched their every move, his ear tufts on full display as he bobbed up and down, turning his head in almost a complete circle. "Have a seat on the loading chute. If you run, I'll shoot." There was a seriousness in Sierra's voice that demanded attention. Nate raised his hands in the air and limped over to the chute. The owl flew off as clouds covered the sun.

Nate Teague was like an albatross to the siblings. From killing their parents to causing Luke's plane crash, to using their land as his own private smuggling route and cemetery, Nate lurked in the shadows, waiting to pounce. Soon it became a dangerous game of cat and mouse between the LaRaes and Teagues that defied all laws of morality. Three generations of trauma collided.

"So, I'll level with you, Nate." Sierra clapped her hands

and Nate flinched. "There's a lot of bad blood between our families and that's why we're here today. We all know how this ends, but we'll treat you with respect and dignity." Nate ran his fingers across his chin. His skinny face and long, lean limbs draped over the loading chute. "How many bodies have you placed on our property?"

"Ten in a mass grave west of the chute here," he said without hesitation.

"Is that all?"

While pointing toward Lake Louisa, Nate mentioned there were three additional bodies off the dock.

Sierra swept the hair from her eyes. "How about guns, weapons, drugs, or any other items stashed here?"

"There's a fifty-caliber ammo can near Cathedral Canyon's west side, containing ghost guns. Also, another one before the aspen stand and spring on the west side of Cutthroat Creek," Nate said, biting his cheek.

Sierra fixed her gaze on Nate like a radar. "Did you kill our parents?"

"My father ordered me to do it because your dad was going to testify against him."

"Are there any other retaliatory plans against our family or nefarious actions in progress?"

"If you hadn't caught me today, I was planning to demolish your family with a car bomb," he said without an ounce of emotion. His eyes taunted Sierra.

"Where's the car bomb, Nate?"

"Under your truck," he said, interlocking his fingers behind his head.

"Is it activated?"

Nate yawned before nodding.

"How much time remains?"

"About five minutes, Sierra."

"So, how do we disarm it?" Luke could tell Sierra was trying to maintain a monotone voice and mask her concern.

"Pull two of the three wires to disarm it. Pull the wrong one and it will detonate. *Boom*," Nate said with emphasis.

"Where did you install it?"

"In the spare tire. I planted the bomb at Paxson Summit when you went back in the morning."

"Luke, watch him," Sierra said as she grabbed her Leatherman and climbed underneath the truck. The Leatherman clicked as she unfolded the pliers, and the sound startled her. When she found the bomb, three minutes remained on the timer. Sierra worked with speed to trace the three wires. She discovered one looped differently and suspected it was a decoy that led back to the actual detonator. With a deep breath, she channeled her intuition. "It's the other two," she said under her breath.

With ninety seconds left on the bomb, she cut the two wires and closed her eyes. When she opened her eyes a second later, she was relieved to see the timer had stopped. Sierra paused, then crawled out from under Luke's truck. Her gaze met Nate's cold blue eyes. After catching her breath, she inquired one last time. "Are there any other surprises you haven't shared with us?"

"So, the bomb was the last one; out with a bang, you know," Nate said, as he cracked a smile.

Sierra gave Luke a curt nod to continue. "Why did you tamper with my plane, Nate?"

"I intended to take you out, one by one. You're like cockroaches and hard to kill, so I had to change my tactics."

Luke spun the cylinder on his revolver like a rattlesnake about to strike. "Anything else you'd like to say?"

"I am a product of my upbringing and my environment. Hate is a learned behavior." His words hinted at self-reflection.

"Did you ever try to leave?"

Nate started to say something then stopped. He shifted his gaze and looked at the ground. "Yes, though my old man clarified that it was me or my siblings; someone needed to carry on the family tradition, so I spared them," he said with raw vulnerability.

Luke locked eyes with Nate and felt his face turning red. "You'll never stop going after our ranch or us, will you?" Nate shook his head.

"How do you want to go out?"

"I'm a modern man with a penchant for tradition, so a single well-placed bullet works for me. I appreciate you both being decent to me. See you on the other side." Sierra met Nate's gaze before signaling Luke to complete the task.

"Any last words?"

Nate shook his head as he glared at Luke. His bloodshot blue eyes pierced him like a cutting torch, carving through flesh until hitting bone. Luke cocked the hammer back on his .357. He walked up and pulled the trigger, hitting Nate between the eyes. Like that, he was gone. All the pain and suffering Nate Teague had inflicted on the LaRae family, and the community of Telford, ended with one bullet. The metallic scent of gunpowder clung to the air, a subtle yet chilling reminder of the lethal consequences that had played out moments before.

Luke cleared his throat. "I thought I would feel better about it. But I almost felt sorry for him."

Sierra leveled a stern gaze at Luke. "This is the same Nate Teague who killed our parents, and almost killed us with a bomb minutes ago," she said, handing him the casing. "He had a hard life, but that doesn't excuse his ruthless pursuit of our family."

They were silent for a moment before Sierra mentioned digging the grave close by, so they could drive over it and pack down the fresh dirt. Luke supported the plan and went to the box in his truck.

"There weren't two shovels before," he said, glancing over his shoulder.

Sierra tipped her cowboy hat, then stored her hat in the truck. Luke handed her his hat and a shovel. When they started digging, a familiar clattering sound echoed as the great horned owl watched from above.

※ ※ ※

When the single gunshot reverberated throughout the canyon, Ruth shrieked. Her younger siblings had carried out the action. This was monumental for the LaRaes: the demise of Nate Teague. She contemplated whether the end of Nate marked another beginning of something else. Her relief soon turned to worry as she and Remy made their way. Ruth, the eldest, preferred being in charge and struggled to let her siblings handle things. To cope, she stayed busy as she tackled the stock water tank repairs.

At the first tank, Ruth discovered two bullet holes, leaking profusely. She dismounted Remy and led the horses to a stand of trees in the shade. Once she secured the horses, she grabbed the supplies from her saddlebag to repair the tank. For a brief moment, she enjoyed her surroundings. While she basked in the sun's warmth, leaves rustled in the breeze as she walked back to the tank. Sunlight peeked through the trees. The scene looked like it was fit for a Bev Doolittle painting with horses concealed in the cover of aspen trees.

After savoring the beauty of the landscape with Koda close by, she checked to see if the plugs would cover the bullet holes. She was in luck; the pre-made wooden plugs would work without needing the drill. So, she swapped her drill for a hammer. The LaRaes have had stock water tanks shot up before and carved some wooden plugs that would expand and fill in the bullet hole. Ruth positioned the plug and drove it in with her hammer. She repeated the sequence of steps on the second hole and the stock water tank was operational again and holding water. With the first repair complete, Ruth gathered her tools and supplies and walked back to the horses.

When packing her saddlebag, she surveyed the meadow. Ruth reflected on the high risk and high reward strategy the LaRaes had been playing for more than a century. She took a deep breath and filled her lungs. "The last few months have given me a greater respect and appreciation for my ancestors," she said, with her eyes searching the horizon. "Also, we LaRaes are ace-high caliber; honest resilient, and, above all, loyal." Placing her foot in the stirrup and grabbing the saddle horn, she pulled herself into the saddle and she was off to tackle the next stock water tank.

The subsequent tank repair was trouble-free, and she made her way back to the horses. She swapped her tools and supplies for her drone equipment. Within minutes, the drone was flying around Cathedral Canyon, sweeping the area and checking for anomalies. She heard cattle and located them in the shade, a couple hundred yards away. While inspecting the herd, she didn't notice any signs of predator activity, like scratches or missing patches of hair. Ruth didn't detect any birds circling above either.

Next, she headed over to Luke and Sierra's location. She could see two figures in the distance who appeared to be shoveling dirt. Ruth descended upon the two. When she was about fifty feet above them, she could see them looking up and waving. They gave her a thumbs-up, so she gained altitude and headed back. While flying back, Ruth spotted a cow elk and her calf. The sound of the drone surprised them, and they stared at the drone like a giant bumble bee buzzing around as she hovered above.

Ruth landed the drone and returned to the horses, then positioned herself closer to the pickup point yet avoided the wide-open spaces. "Nate is dead, but there are plenty of predators," she said, scratching Remy's neck.

***

While it was now late afternoon, the sun was shining in all

its glory, rallying before sunset, with Ruth, Koda, and the horses enjoying the warmth of summer from the trees. As dusk approached, Luke and Sierra completed digging the grave. Drenched in sweat with crusty white salt stains on their shirts and jeans, they made the final improvements and crawled out. Luke and Sierra positioned Nate by the grave. After they lowered him into it, they scrambled out again.

Sierra removed the bomb from Luke's truck and wore gloves before wiping it down with the alcohol wipes from her pocket, then put the bomb on Nate's chest with his arms clutching it. She looked at Luke and dabbed her forehead on her sleeve. "Out with a bang, Nate; the way you had intended."

As Nate gripped the bomb in his cold, dead fingers, an owl hooted in the distance. Luke and Sierra paid their respects before shoveling dirt filled the silence. The shovels clanked under the fading daylight as the subtle, earthy smell of dirt lingered. They finished filling in the grave, and Luke packed down the dirt with the truck and trailer. Once satisfied, he loaded the shovels while Sierra scanned the area with her headlamp. Soon, they headed for Ruth and called to let her know. Sierra looked at Luke. "Do you feel relieved?"

"Revenge isn't as sweet as I imagined. Nate would do anything for his family, and I respect that. When I killed him, it was like holding up a mirror. What he mentioned about hate being learned. That resonated with me, but I don't regret killing him."

Nate is dead. I knew in my bones he would strike today, Sierra thought. He crossed the line when he went after her family. For Sierra, family meant forever, and she vowed to protect them at all costs; there were no limits.

"Also, they say revenge is a dish best served cold." Sierra's venom-laced words sliced through the air like a serrated blade as the trailer thundered down the dirt road. The moon shone through the trees, rising above the day. Their headlights danced over the bumps, illuminating many pairs of eyes scurrying away.

Once they arrived at the pickup spot, Ruth saw headlights in the distance. "Good timing, Remy," she said while dismounting. She loosened Remy's cinch and double-checked Dixie's and Lucky's cinches after loosening them earlier. Luke backed up the trailer and Ruth prepared to load the horses and placed Koda in the cab.

He and Sierra stepped out of the truck, soaked in sweat and covered in dirt. Sierra patted her pants and coughed from the cloud of dust. Their faces said it all. After they exchanged glances, the two unloaded the gear and tools from the saddlebags and placed them in the truck.

With the horses loaded, Luke closed the trailer gate and walked around to the driver's seat. "You want me to drive?"

"Yes, I'd appreciate that," Luke said as he walked around the front and swapped seats with Ruth. Sierra ensured they left nothing behind before departing. Ruth hopped in the driver's seat, moved the seat forward so she could reach the pedals, and adjusted the mirrors. Koda was fast asleep between her and Luke, and Sierra was nodding off in the back seat. The cab smelled tangy, like vinegar. While Luke and Sierra looked exhausted, their eyelids grew heavy from a busy day. "I'm proud of these two," she said in a whisper.

When they pulled into the driveway, Luke and Sierra woke up. Ruth noticed a truck parked by the house, its headlights casting sharp shadows in the dark. "We have company," she said. Luke and Sierra looked at each other with wild eyes and scrambled for guns before Ruth confirmed it was Dirk's truck. "Let's unload the horses, lock your toolbox, and we'll take care of the rest in the morning." Luke and Sierra nodded in approval, and Ruth backed the trailer in near the barn. Ruth informed Dirk they would join him after attending to the horses.

Before they unloaded the horses, Ruth stopped Luke and Sierra. "I'll handle Dirk. What happened today stays at Cathedral Canyon." They acknowledged Ruth as they attended to the horses and tied their reins to the hitching post. Once they put the tack away, they used a curry comb to wipe the sweat off the horses. Sierra walked the three horses to the pasture with plenty of pets along the way while Luke checked their water and Ruth grabbed their feed. The cats peered from the straw bales in the barn, their eyes illuminating the area like marquee lights.

Luke parked the truck and trailer and locked up while Ruth walked toward the house with Sierra not far behind, cradling Koda. Sierra whispered in Koda's ears as she gave her lots of pets. Koda's shrill bark cut through the night.

"Hi, Dirk. Thanks for waiting," Ruth said with a sparkle in her eyes.

"No problem at all."

"Good to see you. We've been worried about you. How are you doing? Will you stay for dinner?"

"I'm better every day, thanks. Sure, I can stay for a bit." Ruth unlocked the door and welcomed him inside. Luke walked into the house with Sierra next. "Looks like you've had a tough day," Dirk said, eyeing the two. They were dirty and stinky. "Yes, we were re-leveling a stock water tank, and it was quite a chore," Luke said. "If you'll excuse me, I'm going to grab a quick shower and then I'll be back." Luke left for the shower. His ripe smell lingered in the air.

Sierra went to shower upstairs after feeding Trixie and Koda. While scanning their pantry, Ruth grabbed some items to make a one-pot dish.

"Where's Gus?" Dirk said as he looked around.

"Coyotes killed him not too long ago."

"I'm sorry to hear that. Who's the new puppy?"

Ruth mentioned Koda is part Australian shepherd and part border collie and a gift from a friend. When Dirk put his hand out, Koda licked him. "How are things, Dirk?" Ruth asked, enunciating her words.

"I'm doing well and stronger each day. Also, Doc Grant was quick to remind me how close I was to not walking away," he said, rubbing his neck.

"I'm glad you pulled through."

There was an awkward pause before Dirk chimed in. "Anything I can do to help; chop veggies or man the pot?"

"If you can brown the skirt steak, I'll chop the veggies." Dirk gave her a thumbs-up before washing his hands and rolling up his sleeves.

Luke walked in and took over chopping veggies and relieved Dirk from the skirt steak. Soon after, Sierra descended the stairs and began setting the table and making lemonade. *I've been thinking about lemonade all day*, she thought. Trixie came to investigate the commotion.

"You have a cat in the house?" Dirk's surprised expression

accompanied his words. They laughed and introduced Trixie, their newest housemate.

While Ruth chopped the bell peppers, jalapeños, and onions, Sierra removed the skirt steak and added the veggies to the cast iron pan. Ruth brought out the flat top for the tortillas. "We're about five minutes out," she said, and everyone nodded with hungry looks on their faces. After taking a seat, they didn't hesitate dishing up a plate. "Thanks for joining us, Dirk. We're so relieved you're on the mend."

"I appreciate you having me." They devoured the steak fajitas and noticed the moon rising while they gazed outside from the dining table. Koda and Trixie were resting on their beds as the medley of cilantro, peppers, steak, and caramelized onions wafted throughout the main level. Soon after clearing the table, they went to the porch.

"So, what brings you by today?"

Dirk lifted his head. "I wanted to thank you for saving my life. You all dropped everything and completed the rescue mission like a special operations team," Dirk said as his voice became pitchy. "Although the Teagues have caused immense pain and suffering, karma comes around. Whatever I can do to help, let me know; no questions asked."

They pondered his words. "Thank you, Dirk. You're like family, and we're glad you called us," Ruth said.

"Nate has been in the wind, and I'll leave it at that. I can't thank you enough." They all took turns hugging Dirk before he drove off into the night. While sitting on the porch, they watched Dirk's red taillights fade into the distance. Luke looked at Ruth. "He knows. So, now what?"

"His loyalty is unmatched, even at great personal

sacrifice. I trust Dirk, and I don't trust many people outside our family." There was an intensity in her eyes; she meant every word.

"Do you think it's over now?" Luke said, leaning back in his chair and observing the dust settle.

"I want to believe that, but reality says otherwise. The Teagues are like cockroaches and hard to kill."

Sierra choked on her drink and almost dropped her glass. "Nate used the same words to describe us."

After a moment of reflection, they let the sound of crickets nearby, in perfect harmony, calm their racing minds.

"It's been a day, and my inner Jack Bauer is showing, so I'm going to call it. Let's have a kitchen confession in the morning to clear the air after chores, irrigation, and, best of all, breakfast and whiskey. Good night." Luke swooped up Koda and went to bed. Sierra realized her Predator long gun and other guns were still in the truck, so she and her sister retrieved them.

Upon returning to the main house, they stored the guns in the safe. Ruth then bid Sierra good night before retiring for the evening. Trixie began meowing as Sierra walked by, and she picked her up.

Sierra returned to the porch, gazing at the stars as a shooting star streaked across the sky. She remembered the events from Lake Louisa. *We're all in, Dad*, she reflected, heading toward the house with Trixie to call it a night. She could still see Braden Harris at the bottom of Lake Louisa and Nate Teague clutching a bomb. Some things are hard to forget.

ELEVEN

Hell or High Water

LUKE FOUND A lead on a Super Cub in Jacks before turning in. As he watched the hours on his alarm clock, he tossed and turned, ready to start the day. He planned to drive up and look at it mid-morning. Knowing they planned a kitchen confession, Luke got an early start. Hell or high water, he would make time for discussion with his sisters, chores, irrigation, and looking at the airplane. When he returned, he'd check the fences at Cutthroat Creek.

By three in the morning, Luke started chores. His headlamp danced as moths flocked to the light. Driving toward the center pivots, he observed the flourishing alfalfa, soon to be harvested. The vibrant smell of alfalfa wafted from the fields. *We're right on track to get two cuttings off the fields,* he thought.

While in the alfalfa fields, he was glad to see the center pivots were operational after the latest round of lightning. In a little over an hour, Luke headed toward the main house to start breakfast. He considered replacing batteries and memory cards in the game cameras on his way back from Jacks. After he parked the four-wheeler, he walked back to the main house with his headlamp still on his head.

It was almost half past four when Luke walked through the front door. He went to the pantry to grab some ingredients. *Pancakes with bacon and a breakfast-style old-fashioned*, he mused. Luke smiled as he whisked the pancake mix and remembered cooking with his mom in the kitchen. With the pancake mix ready, he moved on to cooking the bacon in the cast iron pan. The bacon sizzled in the pan and the aroma of pancakes and bacon filled the kitchen.

When he finished the first batch of pancakes, he piled them on a plate and began another batch, adding blueberries this time. The bacon looked perfect; crispy but not rubbery. Luke set the table and brought the first stack of pancakes, followed by three breakfast-style old-fashioned drinks. After he put the bacon and pancakes on the table, Ruth and Sierra appeared downstairs.

"The chores and irrigation are done, so we can enjoy breakfast." Ruth and Sierra rubbed their eyes and grabbed a seat at the table while Luke placed the maple syrup. When Koda and Trixie came around the corner yawning and stretching, he grabbed their food. "I found a lead on a Super Cub in Jacks. By starting early, I carved out time for our kitchen confession, checking out the plane, and then inspecting the fences at Cutthroat Creek. Anyone interested in going to Jacks? I'm planning to swap out the last game cameras as well."

"I'll go with you, Luke," Sierra said, raising her hand.

"Also, the alfalfa looks like it will be ready to swathe in the next week."

"Great, and thanks for the update. You're on a roll today."

Ruth summarized the weather. Since the triple digits ended after another day, they planned to move the cattle then. Once they finished cleaning up after breakfast, the siblings sat down.

Like previous campfire and kitchen confessions, they started at the beginning. Sierra kicked things off. She explained she felt Nate Teague would try something yesterday. He was becoming more emboldened and desperate. The night before Cathedral Canyon, she went down to the safe and studied the maps of current and potential burial locations and strategized options. That night, she dreamed of an owl. Whenever Sierra encountered an owl, whether in dreams or in reality, death ensued. So, she packed more tools and equipment, including the Predator long gun outfitted with a suppressor, and an extra shovel. After they went their separate ways, she could sense Nate's presence by the silence when trekking up to the vantage point. Before long, she had seen Nate sleuthing near the creek.

Much to her surprise, he had spotted her and sprinted for the trees before she shot him. Once she and Luke arrived at their destination, they untied Nate and removed the gag. He was a monster, though she believed in treating people with respect and dignity, which was passed down by their Great-Grandpa Lee.

After she interrogated Nate on a range of questions, she felt he was being honest in responding. He admitted to killing their parents because their dad was testifying against his father, like Bob Waite had shared. Also, he confessed to putting a car bomb in the spare tire of Luke's truck. A car bomb, of all things. She defused it and removed it from the truck. Yet what stayed with her from yesterday was Nate's admission that he was a product of his upbringing and environment. Sierra gave a quick nod to Luke to take over.

Luke tilted his head at Ruth. "While we found closure with Sierra's help, we also learned about a mass grave, more bodies at Lake Louisa, and an ammo can. Oh, I almost forgot to mention that Sierra had the idea of burying Nate with the bomb." There was a depth of emotion in Luke's expression, as if he were experiencing it all over again.

Ruth tucked her chin. "That's a new twist. When did he place the bomb?"

"After Luke and I returned to handle the bodies at Paxson Summit. Nate mentioned we were tough to kill like cockroaches, so he went with a bomb."

"At least it's done. Nate Teague won't pursue us anymore," Ruth said with a loud sigh.

"Although he might haunt us."

Ruth closed her eyes while she considered Sierra's statement. "Do you feel relieved, Luke? Now that Nate's gone?"

"Not as much as I expected. I worry about what's next."

"Like Amy Bartol's line, the evil you know is better than the evil you don't?"

Luke held his head, deep in thought, as he stared at the

meadow. *I can't tell Ruth I see Nate's gaunt face every time I close my eyes.*

From his drained expression, Ruth sensed he didn't want to elaborate further, and left things alone. There was an awkward silence before Sierra raised her glass and they toasted.

Rather than sit with uncomfortable emotions, the three kept themselves busy. Luke suggested putting equipment away and cleaning out the truck. They knocked it out together. Luke unhooked the trailer while Sierra opened the bay doors of the shop. Ruth gathered the cleaning supplies in the shop, including the caddy with Luminol and a black light. Upon entering the truck, Luke moved the seat back and adjusted the mirrors. When he pulled the truck in, Ruth closed the blackout curtains and Sierra turned off the lights.

The white hazmat suit crinkled as she walked. In a methodical approach, Ruth went through the truck with the Luminol and black light starting on the inside, then working outside. Once she finished, they closed the shop's doors and cracked the truck's windows to let it air out.

With Luke's truck unavailable, Sierra would drive her black F-350. Luke headed back to the main house to gather items for Jacks while Sierra opened the blackout curtains. A strong chemical scent filled the shop. After parking her truck, Sierra grabbed a few items from the house. She came back with her Predator long gun, Colt .32 pistol, some ammo, and her infamous blue backpack.

When she wrapped up, Luke stepped out with a leather satchel and fanny pack. Sierra's laughter sounded like a hyena. Ruth came around the corner and giggled after seeing Luke.

He enjoyed seeing his sisters laugh, even at his expense. Sierra hopped into the driver's seat. "Need anything before we go?"

"I'm good, thanks. I'll take care of the animals, and catch up on some things," Ruth said as she waved goodbye.

✶ ✶ ✶

When they hit the road, Sierra stared at Luke as her hands gripped the steering wheel. "Did Ruth seem distracted?"

"Maybe. We've all had a lot on our minds. I know she feels responsible for Teague's crew taking Dirk. She blames herself, and Caitlin blames her and us, too."

Sierra acknowledged, glancing at Luke and his neon green fanny pack on the seat. "The wildlife must think you're a giant praying mantis or something wearing that thing."

Still shaking her head over Luke's fanny pack, Sierra slowed down before the Telford city limits. A lone raven sitting on a fence post seemed fixated on her. The sun glistened off the raven's blueish-black feathers. He sat motionless, resembling a statue. She gestured toward the raven and Luke lowered his gaze. There was a sense of foreboding surrounding the raven that intrigued Sierra.

When she pulled into the gas station to top off her truck, the raven flew off. Sierra fueled her truck while Luke went to get some items from the store. After she returned the nozzle, a black flash caught her eye. It startled her. Turning, she discovered a raven perched on her hood. The raven observed Sierra with curiosity while holding something shiny in his beak. She sensed the raven's significance and snapped a picture and began recording on her phone. The raven didn't move and continued staring with a fervor that commanded her attention. Once the raven dropped the object, he flew away without turning back.

Sierra picked up the object and inspected it—and was stunned by what she discovered; it was a class ring from Telford High School. The ring, with an emerald stone bearing the year 2023, had the name Hadley Bledsoe engraved on the inside. Hadley was a gifted young athlete well-known in the community. Since she went missing four months ago after hanging out with friends near Telford, there had been no leads. Sierra felt a pit in her stomach. *The raven is trying to show me something. Could it be Hadley*?

While holding the ring, Sierra searched for the raven, but he was nowhere. Luke returned from the store and stopped when he saw Sierra. "Are you okay? You look pale. Like you've seen a ghost."

"A raven landed on my hood and left this ring. It's the class ring of Hadley Bledsoe," Sierra said, hands trembling. "I feel like the raven is trying to send us a message, so let's follow along."

Luke stepped back. He braced himself on the truck as he looked at the ring. "Wow," he said, blinking in excess, still surprised by the discovery.

After a few moments, they jumped into the truck and drove to Jacks with the ring in the cup holder, keeping an eye out for ravens.

"Do you think the raven will lead us to Hadley?" Luke said after clearing his throat. Sierra shrugged and scanned the landscape for ravens. Her stomach churned as she thought about the possibilities of what they might find. When they were almost twenty miles outside of town, Sierra spotted a raven walking around near a tank-trapped road.

She pulled the truck over and parked. Luke stepped out with his .357 revolver inside the waistband of his jeans, and Sierra brought her Colt .32. Sierra glanced over her shoulder at Luke. The raven flew overhead and circled back to ensure they were coming. They were about fifty yards from the truck before Sierra picked up a distinct yet unforgettable smell: decomposition. "Can you smell that?"

The raven circled in one area and cawed as if directing them.

"I can smell something now," Luke said, wrinkling his nose.

As they hiked farther, they could see clothing on the ground in the distance. Their breathing accelerated, becoming shallow and rapid. "It's a body," Sierra said, gasping for air. They kept their distance to preserve the scene and avoid the stench. The body appeared female, and the bright pink Columbia jacket stood out from the vegetation. Sierra plugged her nose then zoomed in with her burner phone to take pictures of the hands. Ravens liked shiny things, so that might explain the peck marks on her fingers.

With her phone, Sierra took coordinates of the location and pictures of the body. She looked at the sky as the raven circled above. *You wanted me to find her. Thank you for trusting me. Why me?* As she shielded her eyes from the sun, she felt lighter, like a weight had been lifted. *You chose me because you knew I listened to animals.* The raven swooped near Sierra and cawed as if in agreement before he flew off and vanished from her view. Although happy to help, she still didn't understand the connection to Hadley. There must be someone close to Sierra related to Hadley. She saw a glimpse of Jake Running Deer when she closed her eyes, and she shivered.

While Luke turned pale and steadied himself against a tree, Sierra seemed captivated, as if she were putting together pieces of a puzzle. "Let's get out of here."

She grabbed a branch off a tree to sweep their tracks, causing a popping sound that made Luke flinch. He led with a brisk pace to the truck. Sierra put the branch in her toolbox and locked it. "I'll call Dirk and tell him the story, minus the raven and the ring."

"You mean you don't want to explain that a raven led you to a body?" Luke said with a half-serious look. Sierra bit her lip. She pulled out her burner phone and called Dirk.

"Hello, Sierra."

"Can you talk?"

"Yes."

"On our way to Jacks to check out an airplane, we pulled over about twenty miles outside of Telford so I could pee. When I walked back from a tank-trapped road for privacy, I smelled decomposition. I'll send you the coordinates and pictures of the body. Will you please keep our name out of it?"

"Of course, an anonymous tip. I'll notify the proper authorities."

"Thanks, Dirk. I appreciate your help," Sierra said as she ended the call. She sent the coordinates and pictures to him through the Threema app.

When Sierra's message arrived, Dirk sat down. He realized the body could be Hadley Bledsoe. She was last reported wearing a pink jacket. Although Telford was a safe community, her disappearance had sent shock waves through western Wyoming. Dirk knew her family and couldn't imagine the pain they were going through.

"You can't make this shit up," Luke said as he took a swig from his flask, trying to drown the memory of the body.

Sierra's eyes widened as she merged onto the road toward Jacks. Luke was quiet. "Are you all right?"

"I'm thinking about Hadley's family. If that's her body, I hope they have the closure they need to move forward."

"I agree. I'm glad we could help." *What's the connection to Jake Running Deer*? she wondered.

Following several minutes of silence, Luke got his phone from his pocket. He called his contact to inform him he would arrive at the hangar in forty minutes. It was a somber ride to the summit. They wound their way up Hermit Pass, and the sun's rays fanned out like tentacles as they crested the summit. *Wyoming has a unique way of drawing you in*.

While they gazed at the scenery, Luke pointed to Gaff Road on the right and mentioned he accessed the game cameras from it. Sierra studied the area and continued down the road. It wasn't long before they pulled into the parking area. "I bet that's my guy," Luke said as he gestured to a slender man with a cowboy hat and handlebar mustache. Soon after, Luke exited the truck and smiled, introducing Sierra and himself.

"I'm Jud Radke," the man said.

"I hope we didn't keep you waiting long."

Jud motioned for Luke and Sierra to follow him. Before going to work, Luke examined the plane and reviewed the logbook. As they talked and walked around the plane, Jud added details about recent maintenance items. Following a short flight, Jud and Luke returned. Both were smiling as they walked away from the airplane.

"I'm asking $180,000 for the Super Cub," Jud said. Luke countered with $170,000 and Jud accepted the offer. They shook hands and Jud completed a bill of sale, while Luke wrote a check for the plane.

"Would you like the check to clear before I take possession?"

"I knew your dad, and I know where your ranch is located," Jud said as he twirled his mustache. Luke had a sheepish grin on his face and Jud handed him the bill of sale and logbook.

"Sierra, would you feel comfortable changing out the batteries and memory cards for the game cameras?"

"Of course. You mentioned you had the locations in your GPS?"

"Yes, let me get it," Luke said as he strolled to the truck. He grabbed his trusty neon green fanny pack and walked to the other side of the truck, where Sierra stood. "So, you can access the six locations through Gaff Road, with a pullout available three quarters of a mile from the pavement."

"Okay, I should be able to handle it, Luke."

"Thanks. I appreciate it. I'll see you back at the hangar."

She waved and looked over the GPS while Luke went to the Super Cub. He called his insurance agent to let her know about the new airplane. Luke prepared for flight while Sierra waited in the truck until he was airborne and waved to Jud.

While Luke flew his new Super Cub, Sierra navigated back to the main road and headed toward Gaff Road. After reviewing the GPS locations, she planned to start with the lower cameras and work her way up. She veered onto Gaff Road and searched for a parking spot. Luke mentioned a pullout about a mile ahead, which is where she parked. Sierra grabbed her Colt .32 and put Luke's fanny pack in her creepy blue backpack. She decided function won out over creepiness.

When reviewing the memory cards, she noticed they were all labeled by camera name, which corresponded to the waypoint names in the GPS. Carrying a water bottle and keys, she locked up and proceeded to the first game camera. As she walked away from the truck, Sierra admired the beauty of the area. "What a serene spot," she said as the melodious sound of songbirds filled the forest.

At six feet tall, Sierra could cover a lot of ground fast, and she was already on the first game camera. She inspected the camera and verified the name before replacing the memory card and the batteries. Soon after, she was hiking again toward the next camera. The second camera went as smoothly as the previous one, and minutes later she reached the last game camera. With the cameras equipped, she headed back. After loading up the truck, she set off to the hangar to retrieve Luke. This was the first time he had been flying since his crash. *Nothing like diving in headfirst*, she considered.

As she approached Hermit Pass summit, Sierra prepared for law enforcement at the pullout. Traffic slowed down, and it was a single lane ahead. While driving in the lane, Sierra noticed several law enforcement vehicles where she and Luke had parked earlier. "Rest in peace, Hadley, and may your family have closure," Sierra said in a low tone.

The heaviness at Hermit Pass persisted long after Sierra found the body. Because the intensity of the situation remained, she reflected on the connection to Jake Running Deer. She was about fifteen minutes from the hangar and called Luke to give him a heads-up. When she arrived at the hangar, Luke came outside. He mentioned he had squared everything away and they could head back to the ranch.

"So, how was the flight?"

He paused and rubbed his throat. "Although I was a little nervous, it came back to me, and I soon forgot about barreling from the sky and crashing into the trees. Each time, I will get more comfortable. Thanks for asking, Sierra."

"Glad to hear it. Like you said, it will take time and today was a major step forward."

They pulled into the driveway before one o'clock, and Sierra parked at the main house. Ruth came out of the house and greeted them. "How did it go?"

"It went well. We have a new plane."

"That's wonderful, Luke," Ruth said, putting her hand on his shoulder. Sierra grabbed the ring and headed toward the house. She met Ruth at the door and handed her the ring. "When did you find this?" Ruth said as her posture stiffened.

"You'll never believe it," Sierra said as she played the video on her phone. "We found a body that could be Hadley Bledsoe."

Ruth brought her fingers to her lips. "Does Dirk know?"

Sierra rotated her head and sat down in a chair by Luke. "Dirk knows."

"You want to talk about it?"

"How about later? Let us update you on the ride up to check the fences."

Ruth hesitated before responding. "We can do that. Thanks, Sierra."

After a dramatic cliffhanger, they began gathering gear to head to the mountains. Ruth brought the barbecue beef sandwiches she prepared for lunch from the fridge and her CZ Shadow 2 handgun. With lunches in hand, Ruth headed toward the barn. Sierra handed Luke his fancy fanny pack with the memory cards and used batteries from her blue backpack.

"I see you're still sporting the creeper bag. Thanks for covering the cameras. I'll put these items in the safe and I'll be right out." Sierra high-fived Luke and paid attention to Trixie and Koda before heading out to her truck. Luke was not far behind. "Need help with the trailer?" He said as he handed her his .357 revolver.

"I'm good, here. Would you mind catching Lucky for me?" Luke agreed and headed off to the barn, and Sierra pulled her truck down to the trailer. While she hooked up the trailer, Luke caught the horses with Ruth. Since Buck was still lame, Ruth took Remy.

Sierra connected to the trailer in no time flat. She grabbed the fencing supplies before backing the trailer in near the barn. Luke and Ruth arrived, leading the horses. Sierra took the lead from Luke, secured Lucky, and went to the tack room.

"I grabbed three fence stretchers, fencing pliers, and hammers, plus smooth wire, staples, and clips," Sierra said, looking over her shoulder toward Luke and Ruth. They both gave her a thumbs-up after wiping the sweat from their faces. With their horses saddled, they swapped the halters for bridles and led them to the horse trailer. Once loaded, Ruth placed her CZ in the gun storage underneath the back seat and handed out barbecue beef sandwiches. "Many thanks, Ruth."

"So, tell me about the ring," Ruth said, tapping Sierra on the shoulder.

While pulling out of the driveway, Sierra admired the beautiful blue sky and warm summer breeze, though her mind was elsewhere, clouded with concern. She recounted the unsettling discovery of the ring earlier that day and what had chillingly followed: finding a body.

"You didn't tell Dirk about the raven or the ring?"

"No, it's difficult to explain."

"I can see that, Sierra. I forget that most people aren't used to interpreting signs from the animal world."

There was an awkward silence before Ruth interjected. "With the possibility of finding Hadley today, do you think we should retrieve Logan's body and relocate it? Like after we move the cows?"

Luke knocked on the dash. "Moving the body is risky. I have the footage where it shows Nate shooting Logan. Although it doesn't describe where the body is located, it shows Nate as the culprit behind his disappearance. We could give this footage to Dirk."

"Also, consider the metadata," Sierra said. "It will provide the geographic coordinates of the footage."

"You both bring up good points. Let's mull it over," Ruth said and then trailed off. Despite the majesty of the mountains, they were mesmerized by the latest revelations and deep in thought. "With bodies in a mass grave by the loading chute and in Lake Louisa, I wonder who these people are."

"Though that's an excellent question, we may not want to know. We've opened Pandora's box once already," Luke said with a stern look.

"Before we act, let's agree to have further discussion," Ruth said as her words lingered like a wind chime in a light breeze. They all supported the plan. An air of contemplation filled the cab the rest of the ride up. Yellow jackets buzzed out the window and the stickiness of the air signaled thunderstorms. Like the raven earlier, an ominous dark cloud descended upon the McGrath Valley.

TWELVE

Hold Your Horses

AS SIERRA PULLED into Cutthroat Creek and positioned the trailer, a cloud of red-winged blackbirds emerged from the trees; their distinct call filled the area like a symphony of chirps and trills. "Grandma Sally loved red-winged blackbirds and believed they were a sign of good luck and protection," Luke said with a sense of nostalgia. He smiled while watching the blackbirds and hearing their high-pitched call. In the dappled light, the sun's rays splintered through the trees and cast a warm glow in the meadow from where he stood.

While enjoying the sun's warmth without roasting, they stepped out of the truck and began setting out their gear. Sierra was out first and opened the trailer gate with Luke ready for the handoff. They secured the fencing supplies to their saddles and in their saddlebags, then tightened the cinches and climbed into the saddles. Sierra led the pack, opened the barbed wire gate, and closed it after they all went through. The three continued to skirt the trees, avoiding being out in the open. Despite Nate being below ground, they were still cautious.

After ten minutes of riding, Ruth looked at Sierra and Luke and gestured to the sky. After dismounting Remy, she walked over to a tree and secured Remy's reins, and then grabbed the drone, battery, and remote controller from her saddlebag. When the drone was airborne, Ruth scanned the area and flew counterclockwise along the fencelines. "Near the aspen on the west flank. The fence is down. It could be the spot where Nate buried an ammo can."

"I can cover that side. I brought a small shovel," Luke said.

"Once I finish this pass, I'll update you on the condition of the fence on that side." Luke watched the display screen while Ruth operated the drone. "There's another small section before the southwest corner, Luke."

"Sounds good, thanks. I'll head that way."

"Meet here in two hours." Luke gave Ruth a thumbs-up. Sierra waited to see how the north flank looked before heading out. The low battery warning on the remote controller went off, so Ruth landed the drone, replaced the battery, and proceeded on her path. The gentle hum of the drone was soothing as it glided across the sky. So far, there was one small area to repair near the northeast corner.

Before finishing the section, she found one more spot to fix before the northwest corner. "I'll take this repair, if you want to grab the one by the northeast corner?" Sierra waved as she and Lucky made their way to the first section of fence and Ruth wrapped up flying the drone. Soon after, she landed the drone and packaged it for transport, then walked over to Remy and pulled herself up in the saddle. Ruth planned to check the stock water tanks on her way up to the northwest corner.

After she arrived at the first stock water tank, the overflow was functioning, and the second tank was also operational. The sun was still shining mid-afternoon and Remy's black mane glistened in the sunlight as he climbed onto the bench toward the northwest corner. On the bench, she could see the fence line and she noticed the broken section. When she reached the location, she dismounted Remy and tied the reins around a tree in the shade while she grabbed the fencing supplies. Ruth was methodical in repairing the fence, taking precautions to ensure her repairs would hold up. Despite her careful approach, she ripped open the flesh between her thumb and index finger on barbed wire. "You'll have that," she said in an unconcerned tone.

Once Ruth completed the repairs, she walked back to Remy and was preparing the fencing supplies for transport when she heard a horse coming down the next bench. She looked up and noticed it was Sierra. Ruth waved as she swung her leg over the saddle. Together, they made their way back to the meadow. When they saw Luke leading Dixie from a distance, not on the saddle, they didn't hesitate to act.

"Let's go," Ruth said, and she and Sierra galloped toward them.

"What happened, Luke?"

"Dixie stepped wrong, and she's limping." Luke's expression was strained, and his voice sounded faint.

"Let's lighten her load." Luke handed Sierra the fencing

supplies and Ruth his saddle, with Sierra also taking his saddle blanket and the ammo can.

"I'll call the vet to have her meet us at the ranch," Sierra said as she pulled out her sat phone. "Kensie, it's Sierra LaRae. Luke's horse Dixie stepped wrong, and she's limping. Can you meet us at the ranch? We're a couple of hours out." Kensie confirmed she'd be at the ranch in a couple of hours.

They rode back to Sierra's truck in silence and unloaded the supplies and put Luke's tack in the back seat. Sierra loaded Lucky and Remy. Luke hung his head, seeing the pain in her eyes as he loaded Dixie into the trailer. He stroked Dixie's mane, trying to comfort her. After he secured her in place, he shut the trailer gate and got in the truck. Luke's concerned gaze made Ruth and Sierra go silent. Ruth put her hands on Luke's shoulders. Sassy but dependable, Dixie had been a rock for Luke, and seeing her injured was hard to stomach. "Kensie is a great vet. We're getting her the care she needs as soon as possible."

Luke let out a loud sigh. "Dixie is the Doc Holliday to my Wyatt Earp, and it crushes me to see her like this." Worry lines creased his sisters' brows as they fretted over him. Losing Gus had been a crushing blow, and Dixie's injury reopened the gaping wound.

While concerned for Luke, Ruth was glad she had met with Jake Running Deer and bought another horse, Misty. However, she didn't plan on two horses being injured at the same time. Jake would arrive tonight with Misty, and she would share the news then.

Tension filled the truck as they drove to the ranch, with Luke clenching the steering wheel. When they arrived, he backed up the trailer and jumped out to unload Dixie. Ruth brought water and feed for Dixie while Luke led her into the barn. Sierra took care of Remy and Lucky and walked them to their pasture. After returning, she grabbed Luke's tack from the truck and put it away. Before parking and unloading the fencing supplies, guns, and ammo can, she heard a vehicle hit the cattle guard - it was Kensie Nelson pulling up to the barn.

Ruth and Luke waved and greeted her. Kensie brought her X-ray machine and began laying out her gear. She did an exam on Dixie's front leg and commented on how warm it was to the touch, showing inflammation. She took X-rays and then brought her laptop over to view the results. Kensie explained she saw no breaks, but suspected a pulled muscle. Dixie would need time to recover. Luke's posture relaxed when he heard the news. "I'll give her pain relief and return to check on her in a couple of weeks. Let me know if her condition changes," she said.

"Can you spare a moment to examine Buck? I think he has a stone bruise, so I've been letting him heal up."

"Of course, Ruth." After grabbing a halter, Ruth caught Buck in the pasture and brought him to the barn. Kensie picked up his foot and started examining it. "I'm not seeing anything that stands out, and based on the tenderness limited to one area, I'd agree with you on a stone bruise. Keep doing what you're doing with him, and he should rebound fast."

Ruth thanked Kensie for checking Lucky as they walked back to Luke and Sierra.

"I appreciate you coming here, Kensie. I've been worried about Dixie." Kensie gave Luke a big hug and mentioned she was always happy to help the LaRaes. Her eyes twinkled and her cheeks blushed. Kensie and Luke had dated in high school. Luke wasn't ready to settle down, so they went their separate ways, yet they remained friends despite Kensie marrying his former best friend, Blaine Nelson. It hurt Luke when Blaine and Kensie began dating. He expected Blaine to inform him in person, not via Facebook. Luke considered Blaine's failure to tell him a betrayal and their friendship had never recovered. Although he was easygoing and good-natured, Luke valued loyalty above all else, and if a person crossed him, it was a life sentence in his book.

Grudges aside, Luke still cared for Kensie. He and Ruth helped her pack up her gear and then waved goodbye. If Kensie and Blaine didn't work out, Luke would swoop in without hesitation. *She's the one who got away, and it's my fault*, Luke pondered as he kicked the dirt. Kensie peeled out in a cloud of dust, but then another truck and trailer showed up unexpectedly. "Hey, isn't that Jake Running Deer's outfit, Ruth?"

"While you and Sierra were checking out the airplane and cracking unsolved mysteries, I met Jake to look at a horse. This is our newest horse, Misty."

Luke stared at Ruth, his mouth agape. "So, how did you know?"

"It seemed like we needed another horse and things came together," she said.

Jake parked near the barn and exited the truck. "Hello, Luke." Jake noticed Luke's bloodshot eyes. "What's going on?"

"Hi, Jake. Dixie stepped wrong today. Although she's okay, she's out of commission for a while. I've been worried about her."

"I understand, and I'm glad Dixie will be all right. This is Misty. She's a magnificent horse and I think you all will love her. So, how's Koda?" Sierra walked around the corner holding her. Jake went to Koda, and she squealed with excitement. After the squeals and puppy kisses, Jake opened the trailer gate and unloaded Misty, a stout, bay mare about fifteen hands with a black mane and tail.

"She looks great, and she's strong," Luke said, stroking her mane.

"Do you want to ride her?"

"For sure." Luke took the halter and lead from Jake, then tied them together to make a rein. He jumped onto her back with ease. Within seconds, Luke was riding Misty. He took her for a quick ride and came back, clapping.

"Though I'm sad about what happened to Dixie today, I like Misty. Good job, Ruth," Luke said. Jake, Ruth, and Sierra exchanged glances and nodded in approval. As they watched Luke on Misty, it reminded them of him riding his red roan pony, Strawberry, when he was six. He had a way with horses, and it was thrilling to watch. While looking at Jake, Ruth remembered she had made enchiladas.

"Jake, would you join us for dinner? I made homemade enchiladas."

"Of course. Thank you, Ruth."

They headed back to the house while Luke led Misty to the barn. He put her into the corral near the other horses, which approached her as if they sensed her belonging. Even Dixie was on her best behavior. *Must be the pain meds*, he mused. Misty would stay in the corral overnight to acclimate and still have access to food and water. When he arrived back at the house, he could hear Koda's shrill bark.

It was a little after six o'clock. Dinner was underway at the LaRaes' house with their guest, Jake Running Deer. The enticing smell of enchiladas and peach cobbler filled the kitchen. Jake enjoyed the company and played with Koda while Trixie slept. The clanking of glasses and silverware, fragrant foods, and beautiful dishes added to the relaxing ambience.

* * *

Soon after dinner and clean-up, the group transitioned to the porch to enjoy the breathtaking sunset. Sierra and Ruth leaned in, sensing Jake's change in demeanor. They noticed his kind eyes were dull and the corners of his mouth turned down. "The authorities think they found Hadley Bledsoe today." The siblings squared their shoulders toward Jake. "She was like a granddaughter to me. My son, Tristan, is dating her mother."

Sierra felt sick. *The reason she saw Jake's face near the body became clear: The raven used her to bring closure to Hadley's family.* She reached into her pocket and presented the ring to him. "I'm sorry, Jake. If I knew she was your granddaughter, you would have been my first call."

"How did you find this?" Jake said as he gripped the ring in his palm.

Sierra told him about how the raven led them to the body, then she played the video from the gas station.

Jake stood up, and Sierra as well, and he hugged her. "The raven trusted you, knowing you would do right. Thank you, Sierra. I have a family meeting tonight about Hadley in Telford, but I will not share this information." Jake gestured to her phone. "Will you show me the photos?" When Sierra pulled up the pictures, Jake clutched his heart. "That's Hadley. My wife and I bought her that jacket." Tears streamed down his face. Sierra felt his pain. Losing family was something she and her siblings could relate to. *It never gets easier*, she thought.

"I'm so sorry, Jake," Sierra said, with tears welling up in her eyes.

Jake put his hand on her shoulder. "You couldn't have known, Sierra. Thank you all for helping bring closure to everyone who loved Hadley." His voice broke with emotion as he looked at them. "Please know that I love you all like family, and I know you'll take wonderful care of Misty."

Tears glistened in his eyes as he pulled Sierra, Luke, and Ruth into a tight embrace. After a long moment, he stepped back, clearing his throat. "I need to go to the family meeting," Jake said.

They all waved goodbye, and he stepped into his truck and headed for town.

With the dust billowing from Jake's truck and trailer, guilt set in. "I feel terrible. I didn't know that Hadley was his granddaughter," Sierra said. Her voice sounded gritty, like sandpaper. Before Ruth or Luke could respond, Sierra grabbed her notebook from the house and started sketching. "I'm adding a raven to my latest tattoo design to honor Hadley."

Everyone copes with grief in their own way, and Sierra channels her emotions through art, Ruth contemplated. Luke and Ruth exchanged glances and continued to watch the colorful sunset unfold and calm their racing minds. Fireflies flittered across the porch, creating an impressive light show. The randomness of the fireflies provided a welcome distraction. After looking around, Luke stood up and turned toward Ruth and Sierra.

The tension ran high, so Luke made a break for it. "I'm going to check on Misty to see if she's doing all right," he said and walked toward the barn as a sea of orange, red, and purple hues dominated the sky. When Luke returned, he pulled up a chair by Ruth and Sierra. "Are you up for moving the herd tomorrow?" They gave a slow nod. The siblings discussed chores and agreed to be on the road before six o'clock.

Luke mentioned he planned to review the rest of the game camera footage before calling it a night. After bidding good night, Ruth remained on the porch, lost in thought. *From taking out a cartel kill squad, rescuing Dirk, and unearthing more family secrets, to neutralizing Nate Teague. What's next*? She stared at the cloudless black sky punctuated by stars, and found comfort in the darkness. Rather than stay on the freight train chugging with raw emotions, she detoured into the kitchen and prepared lunches for tomorrow.

✱ ✱ ✱

While Luke reviewed the game camera footage, he made an astonishing find—Tristan Running Deer loading his backpack with white bricks he presumed were drugs. Luke felt a knot growing in his stomach. He remembered Jake mentioning that his son, Tristan, dated Hadley's mom. He shook his head in disbelief. "I need to tell Jake. There's been too much pain today," he said, covering his eyes with his hands. "I feel nauseous." His voice sounded strained. *I'll let him know tomorrow after we move cows*, he reasoned. Despite calling it a night, he was far from sleepy. His mind agonized over his latest find and sharing more upsetting news with Jake.

Before sunrise, they prepared to move the herd. Luke unhooked Sierra's truck from the trailer and attached his. While Ruth checked the irrigation, Sierra gathered items from the house. Luke and Sierra saddled the horses. Ruth returned and within fifteen minutes, they loaded the horses and were on the road to Cathedral Canyon. "Good morning, everyone," Luke said with sleep still in his eyes. It was now a quarter till six o'clock.

"I called Uncle John last night, and he and Aunt Ronnie will bump our truck and trailer around."

"Great catch, Ruth."

Sierra tapped her siblings on the shoulder. "I brought a rifle and handgun for everyone. They're stored underneath the seat. Also, thanks for making lunch, Ruth." Luke had some news to share with his sisters about what he found on the game cameras, though he noticed Sierra's jumpiness, and he held off on his update. Sierra pulled on her shirt collar as she cleared her throat.

"So, I received word late last night that they're releasing Wes Wood from prison today." Ruth raised her fingers to her mouth as she heard Sierra's words. "I'm sorry, Sierra. He put you through hell and to think his dad was a county commissioner." Luke pounded his fist on the steering wheel.

Her voice quaked. "He will come after me again; I know it." Wes was a bully and Sierra blamed his dad for him becoming a monster. Five months after their parents passed away, Wes became obsessed with Sierra, and she suspected he was stalking her. Sierra's mind raced as she recalled that fateful day when Wes revealed his true colors.

***

It was a vulnerable point in her life after her parents died, and Wes used it as an opportunity to prey upon Sierra. He killed her orange cat, Fluffy, when she refused to go to prom with him, though she could never prove it. However, the final straw for her was when he attacked her after trapshooting practice. She could feel someone watching her at the range, and she was on guard. Unbeknownst to Wes, she was not alone that day: Zeke Adams was there, too. Zeke was an advisor for trapshooting, and he was helping Sierra perfect her technique.

"I remember Wes hit me over the head with a metal pipe. Zeke emerged and jumped on him. I escaped and then I heard a gunshot. Not knowing who got shot, I grabbed the pipe. Wes shot Zeke, so I blasted him with the pipe. I snatched the gun and called 911, but Zeke was gone."

Brushing her thighs with her fingers, Sierra recalled testifying against Wes in court. He mouthed the words, "You're dead, bitch," when she was on the stand. Since Wes had turned eighteen before the incident, they tried him as an adult. He received ten years in prison without parole. Wes had all the traits of a serial killer, making it challenging to envision his current state.

✴ ✴ ✴

With her voice still shaky, Sierra looked at her siblings and said, "He won't waste any time in coming after me. I'll be ready, but I'll need your help to take him down."

"Anything and everything you need, Sierra," Ruth said as she grabbed her hand. When they were young, she and Ruth adopted that credo, *Anything and Everything*. Knowing her sister remembered it meant the world to her.

"You got it, Sierra," Luke said, staring intensely at her in the rearview mirror.

Sierra's voice gained strength, like she was taking back her power. "We'll be prepared for Wes. His father is his only family left, but he'll be residing at the halfway house in Telford. My worst fear has materialized: Wes will be out there beyond the prison walls. And he's had a decade to plot his revenge," she said, her voice trailing off.

"Let's plan it out and then execute, in more ways than one," Luke said as he made a gun with his thumb and index finger. They all nodded in agreement as they arrived at Cathedral Canyon and Luke backed the trailer in.

"Despite the chaos, let's prioritize moving cows today. We must stay focused and not let this news distract us to keep our animals and us safe." Luke and Sierra gave Ruth a thumbs-up and everyone took a deep breath.

After they positioned the trailer, they left the truck and proceeded to the back. Luke led Misty out first, and then Sierra and Ruth brought Lucky and Remy. Sierra tied Lucky to the grille guard of the truck while she doled out guns and lunches to Luke and Ruth. Soon after tightening her cinches, Sierra threw her leg over the saddle, and they were off.

The golden rays spilled across the landscape into sharp slivers, highlighting the three silhouettes on horseback. Ruth dismounted Remy and launched her drone to look for the cattle. Everything seemed fine while flying the area and she packed up the drone. They approached the trees and rode through the cattle. One steer calf had claw marks on his back. "A mountain lion's work," Luke said, pointing at the calf.

Upon reaching the meadow, Sierra took point and opened the gates. Ruth closed them at the drag position in the back and gathered any stragglers. Luke rode in the middle covering swing and flank, floating where needed between his sisters. When they progressed to the southwest corner, Sierra loped ahead to open the first gate and returned with plenty of time to spare. Luke and Ruth worked out a plan: if they needed to rope an animal, Ruth would handle the roping since it was Luke's first day riding Misty.

Spot, the matriarch cow, with a large white circle on her face, took the lead. She settled into a steady pace, and a few different bunches began forming.

Loud crashing and banging followed by cattle bawling

filled the canyon. Two black angus bulls were pushing each other around. When the fighting escalated, Ruth roped one bull around the head on the first loop, dallying the rope, wrapping the other end of the rope around her saddle horn to secure it, and adjusting the slack. Remy did an excellent job of bringing the bull along. Ruth loosened her rope to add slack, flicked her wrist, and popped it off the bull's head. The bull returned to the herd and fell in line as she finished coiling her rope back up and placing it on her saddle.

Sierra watched the herd from a distance to guide them toward the loading chute. She drove the cattle over Nate's grave and turned the herd. Spot led, followed by the rest of the cattle in a long, dusty line. It was almost eight o'clock when the sun reached Cathedral Canyon, bringing light to the valley of darkness where so many secrets lay buried.

While the cattle trampled by the loading chute, right beneath their hooves, Nate Teague lay hidden. Sierra looked up at the sky and thanked her dad. The sound of hoofbeats and saddle leather filled the silence. They let the cattle settle into a rhythm without pushing the pace. Their primary concern was the safety and wellbeing of the animals, with the whole day available for them to travel to Cutthroat Creek. The three continued to assess the herd and planned to get water before the final push at Lentern Lake. As Sierra led the herd, she heard a horse coming up behind her. It was Luke, and she scanned his face for clues.

"Hold your horses. Everything is all right, Sierra. I wanted to check to see if we're still planning to water the herd at Lentern Lake."

"Phew." Sierra took a deep breath. "Yes, same plan."

Luke rode beside her, and she turned her head toward him. "So, how's everything going with you and Ruth?"

"It's going well. We have three larger bunches and several smaller ones, though the cattle look well, and I'm not seeing any sore feet or anything."

"Excellent. Spot's pace remains steady, like a metronome."

Luke wiped the dirt off his face. "I'll head back and we'll see you at Lentern Lake." Sierra waved goodbye as she watched Luke's black cowboy hat fade into the distance, like a tumbleweed on the open plains, rowdy and untethered like Wyoming.

I hope I always live wild and free, Sierra thought as she looked over the landscape and heard the cattle lowing.

THIRTEEN

A Lick and A Promise

SURROUNDED BY TREES, Lentern Lake looked majestic as the sunlight reflected off the surface. Two pairs of trumpeter swans swam near the edge. At six feet long and over twenty pounds, trumpeter swans are the largest waterfowl in North America. The epitome of grace, they glided across the lake with their long, elegant necks and white plumage. However, the beauty of the swans and tranquility of Lentern Lake belied what could lurk beneath the surface. Jaded after Lake Louisa, Sierra wondered if there were bodies there, too. When her thoughts drifted, a stealthy hornet stung her, grounding her back to reality. She cupped her hand over the smarting sting as she looked back at the herd.

With Lentern Lake close by, Sierra prepared to hold the herd up for water. Spot saw the lake and let out a low grumble. She knew where she was going. Sierra laughed and petted Lucky. The herd slowed down with Spot leading them to the water. As the cattle filed in for water, Sierra backed off to give Lucky a chance to drink.

The sun cast a fluorescent glow from the highest point in the sky. Squinting from the sun, Sierra saw Luke making his way toward her location. "Howdy," Luke said with a dirt mustache and caked-on eyebrows. They caught up on small talk as they continued watching the herd while letting their horses drink water.

"I'm going to check on Ruth." Sierra disappeared into the dust, then heard a familiar crash and bang interrupted by cursing. Once she had seen Ruth with the bull, she gave her a wide berth. Like a creature possessed, he leaped and snorted, while Remy stayed cool as an alpine lake in the spring.

Ruth broke right into a clearing before she added more slack in her rope and flicked her wrist to lift it off the bull's head. The bull calmed down. He escaped Ruth and Remy by heading straight to the lake. Puzzled, Ruth glanced at Sierra and said, "Well, that was fun. The gentlest bull in the pasture turns into the biggest jerk during breeding season. Go figure."

Sierra wiped her crusty neck. "I can grab the back if you want to water Remy."

"Sounds good, and thanks," Ruth said as she finished coiling her rope. Luke stayed with the primary group and inched them along the lake while the rest of the herd went to water. Within fifteen minutes, Sierra had twenty head of cattle going toward the lake. When Sierra caught up with her siblings, she asked Ruth if she'd send up the drone to look for stragglers. Ruth agreed and scanned the area, though she didn't find any cattle.

Luke swapped places with Ruth, and she tipped her cowboy hat in appreciation. Lucky's horseshoes clicked as he and Sierra worked their way up to the front, with Spot leading the herd. "One more push," Luke said to Misty as they observed the cows and calves. Ruth found a place near the middle and kept a watchful eye, along with Remy. Luke had ridden far back, doing another sweep for stragglers. Once satisfied, he joined the herd on the final push.

With the gate to Cutthroat Creek ahead, Sierra rode up on Lucky and opened the gate, then returned to the herd. Spot led the entire way, refusing to give up her place, then lowed to the others. She followed Sierra into the gate with ease, with her head held high, and swiped the grass as she continued moving farther into the meadow. When Sierra looked over at the herd and assessed her surroundings, she noticed their truck and trailer parked in the shade and she smiled. The sunlight reflected off the shiny aluminum trailer like a signal mirror. With the gate open and the truck and trailer in place, she returned to the herd to assist Ruth and Luke.

"I can see glimpses of Luke in the distance, so I'll fly the drone to check things out."

"Copy that, Ruth," she said while heading back toward Luke. Within ten minutes, Sierra had caught up with Luke and he had about fifty head of cattle with him. "Ruth is flying the drone to check for stragglers. I'll do another sweep if you take them the rest of the way." Luke took his cowboy hat off and waved her on.

Sierra continued working her way further and weaving through the trees, looking for more cattle. She heard the buzzing above and spotted the drone. With a mischievous look, Sierra imagined other uses for the drone and chuckled. *Oh, the potential,* she mused. After exploring the timber, she climbed to a vantage point and surveyed the surroundings. She could still hear the drone humming. It was hovering fifty feet above her head, and when she gave a thumbs-up, the drone gained altitude and flew off. Sierra petted Lucky as they made their way back to the meadow and joined her siblings.

While they rode together to check the stock water, Sierra looked at Luke. "So, what did you find on the rest of the game cameras?"

Luke became fidgety and avoided eye contact. "Let's finish up and I'll update you later."

"Okay," Sierra said, sensing his discomfort and changing the subject. "How did Remy do?"

"He's incredible and did a terrific job of handling the bulls and letting me rope off him."

Ruth rode over to Luke. "How's Misty doing?"

Luke bit his lip and tapped his saddle. "She's a great mare and a smooth traveler, for sure."

"Out with it, Luke."

"Not until we get to the truck. Because I need to keep my wits about me until we're done here."

"All right, then Sierra or I will drive back."

Luke nodded in agreement.

With the first stock water tank functional and the second, they let their horses grab a drink. Before leaving, they spread out and examined the herd for pinkeye, abscesses, lameness, or other health issues. They returned and exchanged updates, then made their way to the truck. Luke grabbed the gate.

Chipmunks chattered in the distance as they rode by. They surveyed the herd, relieved the cattle drive went off without a hitch. *The day isn't over yet. Wes is still lurking,* Sierra pondered. She grabbed her stiff saddle strings and twirled them around her fingers in haste.

At the truck, Sierra dismounted Lucky and grabbed her guns. She noticed a cooler in the front seat and smiled like the Cheshire cat. Luke walked up and handed her more guns. Sierra loosened Lucky's cinches and led him into the trailer and then swapped places with Ruth. While Sierra sat in the driver's seat, Ruth handed Luke a sandwich and a lager from a Wyoming brewery. Luke smiled and raised his beer in the air. The clanking of cold beers and a pop for Sierra lingered as they thought about their Uncle John and Aunt Ronnie.

With a pop in her hand, Sierra pulled onto the road with the sun peeking through the trees like cries for help, hinting at what happens after dark. The name Cutthroat Creek has a rich history from the area's earliest settlers. In the 1880s, Wyoming was an untamed frontier where even Cutthroat Creek lacked sanctity. A feud between rival homesteaders resulted in one of them cutting the throat of the other by the light of the full moon, giving rise to the name Cutthroat Creek.

The area was also the scene of Ruth's bear attack that killed her horse, Ace. Despite its allure and unmistakable beauty, there was a baleful undercurrent that set in after nightfall. The area glowed with eyes, giving the unshakeable feeling of being watched. "Remember when we were riding here, working on the stock water, a couple of years ago? We counted twenty pairs of eyes riding back."

"I remember that, Ruth, and it inspired me to put the timber wolf tattoo on my arm to signify the power of the pack."

"Of course," Luke said, slapping his leg. Dust flew everywhere, as he coughed.

"All right, Luke, now that you're in good spirits again, tell us about what you found on your game cameras."

Luke collected his thoughts. "I have a video of Tristan Running Deer talking about smuggling drugs in Jacks to rich people and more footage of him packing and loading bricks into his backpack."

"You're sure it's him?"

Luke nodded and ran his hands through his hair. "So, we need to tell Jake."

"What do you think about calling Jake to see if he's near Telford?"

"That could work. I want to tell him in person and show him the footage."

Ruth cleared her throat. "Let's call him from a burner after we get into service again." Luke exhaled as he watched the sun descend.

Once they cleared the final switchback, Ruth powered on her burner phone. "Do you want to call Jake, or would you like me to?"

"I will, thanks." Ruth handed him her phone, and he called Jake. Before the second ring, Jake answered the phone. "Hi, Jake, it's Luke LaRae. I'm sorry to bother you. We're driving back from moving cattle today and I have some information to share with you. Are you around Telford?"

Before responding, Jake hesitated. "I'm still in Telford."

"Would you meet us at the ranch in the next couple of hours?"

"I'll be there. Thanks, Luke," Jake said and ended the call.

Luke filled in his sisters and mentioned Jake would join them for dinner and strong drinks in a couple of hours. Luke added the second part, but they didn't object. While chasing the sun, the three made it back to the ranch and noticed Dirk's truck parked at the house and him walking down to the barn.

"Good to see you, Dirk."

"Quick update. Wes Wood is staying at a halfway house on Fifth Street in Telford. Also, the body is Hadley Bledsoe." They shook their heads and scanned the area before Sierra spoke up.

"Thanks, Dirk, for letting us know about Wes and Hadley." Sierra's voice was monotone. "Although I knew this day would come, it didn't make it any easier. I appreciate your help in handling the body we came across. At least her family will have closure now."

"Wes is planning to come after you, Sierra. He hasn't changed and he might even be worse than before. Let me know if I can help."

"Thanks for making the trip, Dirk. I'll let you know if we need help."

"Since my in-laws are visiting, I should get back."

Luke and Ruth joined in and waved goodbye as Dirk strolled back to his truck. Sierra turned with fiery eyes after they exchanged glances. "Tell him I'm coming, and hell is coming with me."

"I'm in, Sierra, and I always appreciate quoting Wyatt Earp."

With an air of confidence, Ruth made pistol gestures. "Count me in with both guns blazing."

In a single look, they communicated their task: Eliminate Wes.

Once they broke eye contact, the siblings turned toward the trailer and unloaded the horses. Luke walked Misty out. Next, Sierra brought out Lucky and Remy, while Ruth checked on Buck before returning to the barn. With care and diligence, they unsaddled the horses and brushed off the sweat before rubbing down their legs.

After swapping their bridles with halters, they gave the horses lots of pets as they took them to their pasture and released Misty with the herd. Luke watched as Dixie moved toward Misty and whinnied in a low register before nuzzling her. His eyes widened as he did a double-take, and he appreciated Dixie making the effort. Before he walked back to the barn, he checked the trough along the way. Luke could hear the barn cats meowing while Sierra fed them, and Ruth parked the truck and trailer. They strode to the truck, grabbed the gear and guns, then returned to the main house.

When they opened the front door, Trixie and Koda greeted them. Luke picked up Koda and Sierra swooped up Trixie and they cuddled their furry friends before getting them dinner. "We have about an hour before Jake will arrive, so here's a lick and a promise approach to dinner: shepherd's pie, sourdough bread with rosemary garlic sauce, and banana pudding parfaits," Ruth said.

Luke and Sierra clapped in approval.

While they put the guns back in the safe before heading upstairs to shower, Ruth charged her drone batteries and remote controller. Moments later, she started dinner. With the shepherd's pie cooking and the banana parfaits chilling in the fridge, Luke walked down the stairs and could smell the aroma of rosemary and garlic.

"What can I do to help?"

"Finish the rosemary garlic sauce from this recipe, set the table, and make strong drinks. Thanks, Luke. I'll shower and return. Shepherd's pie has fifteen minutes left. Banana pudding parfaits are in the fridge."

Luke smiled and rolled up his sleeves. When Ruth went upstairs, she met Sierra coming down. She asked her to coordinate with Luke for the next items on the list. Ruth returned from her shower to find Luke and Sierra had completed the list. The shepherd's pie was on the stovetop covered in aluminum foil to stay warm, and Jake had pulled up to the house. "Impeccable timing, Ruth."

"Hi, Jake, please come in," Luke said as he opened the door and gestured for Jake to enter.

"Hello, Luke, thank you," Jake said and walked into the house, petting Koda and Trixie.

"We have some items to talk about, though our dad always taught us to never discuss important items on an empty stomach, so please join us for dinner."

Jake, with a slight smile and a twinkle in his eyes, said, "Smart man."

Once everyone had eaten to their heart's content, they headed outside to enjoy the evening. Luke refilled everyone's drinks and clinked his fork on his glass before he initiated the conversation. His face became tense, and the cords in his neck stood out. "Jake, thanks for coming out to the ranch. The afternoon before you brought Misty to us, Sierra pulled the memory cards from the game cameras near Jacks while I flew my plane back. When I reviewed the footage, I came across some disturbing video that I want to show you," Luke said as he handed his tablet to him.

Jake maintained a deadpan expression watching the video. "Is there more?" Luke played the second video. After viewing both videos, his posture stooped, and he looked at Luke and paused. "Thank you, Luke. It took a lot of courage to show me the videos. Tristan has been struggling and became involved with the wrong people. A week ago, he confided in me, sharing his concerns about his associates since he wanted to leave. If his suspicions were correct, my son could never live with himself."

Tristan loved Hadley like she was his own daughter. When the authorities confirmed the body found was Hadley, they mentioned there were signs of torture with an "O" carved into her forehead to show the circle of life was complete. The detective described seeing the "O" carving in several cases involving drug trafficking. Devastated from the recent development, Tristan became inconsolable.

"I haven't seen Tristan since yesterday and after reviewing these videos, I'm worried about him. I know his probable location, but flying is the best choice because of the terrain. Would you be willing to help me look for Tristan with your plane?"

Luke stroked his chin. "Of course. Let's go up tomorrow." Jake nodded in approval and stared at the horizon.

They all sat in silence, watching the sunset as if the answers they were seeking would appear. Jake glanced at Luke, inquiring about the hangar meeting time and if he could leave his stock trailer. They agreed on meeting at eight o'clock and leaving his trailer at the ranch.

Jake stood up, addressing the LaRaes. "Thank you all for dinner and for sharing the videos with me. I appreciate your help in finding Tristan." He was shaking and Sierra steadied him.

"I'll help you unhook the trailer," Luke said as he jumped up from his chair and helped him down the stairs. Jake insisted he could drive. Sierra and Ruth hugged him before he and Luke walked to his truck and trailer.

In a quick glance, Ruth noticed Sierra's strained expression. "How are you doing since the news about Wes?"

"I'm…I'm okay and still working through it." Her lip quivered as she considered who else Wes might hurt to get to her.

Ruth watched as Sierra's body betrayed her and revealed subtle inconsistencies. She worried about her sister and began biting her fingernails.

When Luke returned, he noticed the tension and tiptoed up the stairs. Sierra motioned to Luke to grab a chair.

With the three on the porch, Sierra interrupted the sunset viewing with a strategy session. "Before we get straight to tactics, I'll share observations about my crazed stalker, Wes."

Luke and Ruth tilted their heads before they took a drink from their glasses.

Sierra closed her eyes and paused. "Wes is a forceful guy. He is the type who enjoys watching the life fade from his victim's eyes as he chokes them. Also, he's into technology, and I could see him trying to hack into a vehicle using Bluetooth to disable it or cause a crash. Wes has had ten years to think about what he's going to do to me and plan it, so I won't underestimate him or insult his intelligence. He's unstable and has uncontrollable rage, and I suspect he still has these issues and more."

Ruth tapped the rim of her glass. "Are there details we can shore up, like his vehicle or where he's working?"

"He's driving a black 2006 Chevy Silverado extended cab with Wyoming plates and a green Bigfoot bumper sticker, and he works as a dishwasher at Bill's Tavern. Also, his Dad took him to the DMV to get squared away with a driver's license earlier today."

"Did Dirk confirm these details?"

Sierra nodded and steadied her gaze at the horizon after finishing her drink.

"So, what's your gut telling you?" Luke asked, putting his hand on her shoulder.

"He'll strike when he thinks I'll least expect it, like during an everyday activity, feeding the barn cats or horses, for instance. Wes knows I love animals, and I sense he'll go after them to get to me. You both are not safe as long as he's still alive. I'm sorry you're at risk because of me," Sierra said, lowering her head.

Wes's release from prison put the LaRaes on edge. The

threat was imminent. Ruth mentioned with nightfall fast approaching, they should take a cruise around the place with thermal binos and ensure all their security systems were functional. She simulated the security tests and coordinated with Luke and Sierra. All systems were firing, and they proceeded with caution around the ranch. With two pairs of thermal binos, Luke and Sierra went to work glassing their surroundings. "Wait. There's a truck on the main road toward town. It looks like a Chevy Silverado parked with its lights off," Sierra said.

In the binos, Sierra observed a man holding a thermal scope, gesturing as if it were a gun. "It's him," she said as she shivered. Within an instant, the headlights came on, and the truck backed up and then bolted toward town.

"I bet he's going back to meet his curfew before ten o'clock."

"Now we know his intentions and he knows ours," Sierra said.

Ruth signaled to huddle close. "All right, we need to be vigilant, and we can't take any chances. We need a shooter to cover while we do chores and other tasks."

"No chances," Luke and Sierra said in unison.

Sierra's voice sounded pitchy, and Ruth noticed her movements were jerky, like a chipmunk. Ruth's eyes darted around the buildings and equipment, looking for signs of movement. The hair on the back of her neck bristled. Her protective instincts kicked into overdrive as they walked around the rest of the buildings.

Despite a thorough search, they found nothing and went back to the house. The siblings exchanged glances without a single word. They realized it was not if he would strike, but when. It was the calm before the storm. The full moon and still night created a tension that was tangible. An owl hooted in the distance, concealed in the shadows.

I'm taking my life back, Wes. You won't walk away this time, Sierra thought as she opened the front door. There was an intensity about her, like a tea kettle right before it whistled. The slow simmer to redemption had taken years to reach the boiling point.

* * *

Ruth grabbed a glass of whiskey and headed back to the porch. "With Nate six feet under, Wes released from prison, and Luke flying with Jake to look for Tristan, what could go wrong?" she said in a whisper. A shooting star fell from the sky like a rock skipping across a calm lake. Her face felt hot to the touch and her vision became blurry. Ruth focused on her breathing for a few moments and composed herself. "Nothing we can't handle."

FOURTEEN

Burning the Breeze

ASIDE FROM THE wind howling outside and branches scratching against the windows, it was a quiet night. The wind whistled in a chorus of screechy wails and violent bursts.

While her siblings slept, Sierra plotted her attack. By headlamp, she prepared an arsenal and devised a plan to take down Wes. She called it Operation Zero Wes Thirty. Her attempt at being clever at one o'clock or zero one hundred in the morning.

After getting the weapons, Sierra reviewed the maps of current and potential burial sites, and came up with a short list. She also reviewed the "Dark List" resources for neutralizing threats again to ensure they remained front of mind. *It's a one-way trip for Wes with a stop at Colt and Remington*, she thought.

As the Fourth of July neared, more watchful eyes

emerged. The allure of summer in the mountains provided more visitors and opportunities to encounter tourists, backpackers, campers, and others. Wes didn't care who he hurt to get to Sierra, and that worried her. Shivers ran up her spine. Every cell in her body screamed danger. But she plowed ahead without looking back.

With the weapons still laid out on the kitchen table, Ruth and Luke came downstairs. It was four o'clock, and wiping the sleep from her eyes, Ruth looked at Sierra. "Did you get any sleep?"

She shook her head and handed them her plans.

"What are we looking at, Sierra?"

"It's a plan to take out, Wes."

"So, it's a murder map?"

Sierra confirmed Ruth's assumption and moved the weapons, then laid out the documents on the table. She gave them an overview of her assessment. Based on Wes's stalking tendencies, she developed tactical plans. The four most probable locations to intersect with Wes: 1) The ranch; 2) Cutthroat Creek; 3) Cathedral Canyon; and 4) The hangar.

With Luke heading out to the hangar today, she recommended he pack a rifle and handgun and sweep the vehicle before and after for trackers and other devices. In the barn, Sierra would have the best view for chores and irrigation. Luke and Ruth were on board with the assessment and tactics, so Sierra grabbed the thermal binos and her Predator long gun.

"I'll go check it out. If you hear a whistle, come armed," Sierra said, putting the whistle around her neck.

Sierra scanned the house and guesthouse and then

focused on the barn and pastures. It was approaching the twilight phase, when it wasn't light or dark, but in between. As she picked her way to the barn, she glassed the shop, tractors, equipment, vehicles, and trailers, and came up empty.

However, when she made it to the barn, she could smell Marlboro Red cigarettes before discovering one burning on the barn floor. After stomping out the cigarette, Sierra searched the barn. She heard a door slam shut on the road and a vehicle engine revved, gunning it for town.

Through the binos, she recognized it as the truck from last night. Yet, something told her she needed to investigate the barn more. What she found sickened her. Teddy, her beloved orange tomcat, lay motionless with a note written in blood stating, "You're next, bitch."

Sierra waved her fist in the air; disgusted that he hurt Teddy to get to her. She knelt and placed her hand on him. His body felt warm. He hadn't been dead long. With rage in her eyes, her voice shuddering, "Teddy," Sierra said, "I'm so sorry. He will pay."

Rather than let her emotions take over, Sierra detached and focused on Wes's next move. She suspected Wes headed back to the halfway house, so she walked back to meet her siblings. It was now half past four o'clock. Luke and Ruth were on the porch, armed for war, studying her murder map.

Daylight arrived. The sun would rise soon. With a somber expression, Sierra addressed Ruth and Luke.

"I found a cigarette on the barn floor. And saw the truck from last night." Sierra cleared her throat. "I...discovered Teddy, his neck snapped, with a note written in blood, telling me I'm next."

Ruth and Luke jumped up from their chairs with wide eyes and gaping mouths and put their arms around her. "I'm sorry about Teddy," Ruth said as she lowered her gaze. Sickened by Wes's behavior, the siblings considered the atrocity an act of war.

They stood in silence before they went into the house. A sense of foreboding clung to the air like a suffocating blanket. Wes had gone too far and they were going to stop him, once and for all.

After putting their rifles back in the safe, Ruth and Luke kept their handguns as they walked to the barn to start chores and irrigation.

"I'll go back and grab the scanner in case he planted something."

"Oh, *this* scanner?" Ruth said, pulling it from her back pocket. "I checked the porch and found nothing."

As they continued with chores, Sierra scanned the barn. It wasn't long before she discovered a recording device. Another scan of the area came up empty, so she fed the barn cats while waiting for Luke and Ruth. The cats would often greet Sierra, but not today. They were hiding. Still traumatized from the barbarity earlier.

Once they returned, Sierra held her index finger to her lips, her eyes darting with urgency. She motioned for them to approach quietly, and they crept toward her. Moments later, she blew her whistle, the shrill sound echoing in the silence of the barn. In one swing of the farrier driving hammer, Sierra shattered the recording device. She attacked the remnants of the device with ferocity.

The two stood still like pillars of calm amidst chaos, observing a woman pushed beyond her limits.

After she composed herself, Sierra led her siblings to Teddy. Pulling out her burner phone, Sierra took pictures of him and the note. She showed her siblings his broken neck. "Oh, jeez, how cruel," Luke said, turning away.

"That's horrible. We can help bury Teddy."

Sierra lifted her head and nodded.

"Luke and I can dig the hole while you make the cross. What spot are you thinking?"

"By the birch tree," Sierra said, pointing toward the yard.

"Teddy wouldn't hurt a soul. He was so sweet and innocent," Luke said, his voice cracking while he grabbed the shovels.

As Sierra walked to the shop, feelings of guilt sank in. Wiping the tears from her face, she gathered some scrap lumber and began taking measurements and marking the boards before heading over to the miter saw. She put her safety glasses on and then powered on the miter saw, cutting the boards to length. Sawdust sprayed from the saw while the smell of fir lingered.

The whine of the belt sander intensified in the shop, so she wore earplugs to muffle the sound. With the boards sanded and painted, she created a cross and secured the boards with screws. She steadied her hand and painted his name and portrait on the cross.

Sierra showed the cross to Ruth and Luke before wrapping Teddy in a blanket and lowering him into the grave. She stood up again, gazing toward the sky. They all said their goodbyes to Teddy and took turns filling in his grave. Sierra gathered rocks and bit her lip to fight back tears.

With the grave complete, Sierra positioned the cross and used the rocks to anchor it. "Rest in peace, Teddy," she said as she knelt and placed her hand on his grave, her fingers raking the dirt.

After a few minutes, Ruth looked at Sierra. "We're going to finish the irrigation. Will you scan the vehicles?"

With a pained expression, Sierra signaled she would.

Like a marble statue, she stood in complete silence, absent of movement, while staring at Teddy's grave. Moments later, she trudged toward the vehicles. Her steps echoed with sorrow and regret, each one heavier than the last. Ruth and Luke swung by the house and fed Koda and Trixie before heading out. Sierra did a thorough sweep of the vehicles and shop and found nothing, so she walked back to the house to start breakfast. When she opened the front door, Koda and Trixie sensed something was wrong and went to console her. Their kind, understanding eyes helped soothe her frayed nerves.

Since losing Teddy, Sierra craved comfort food and opted to make biscuits and gravy. She went to work on her mother's three-ingredient biscuit recipe with self-rising flour, milk, and cold butter, and once the biscuits were in the oven, Sierra began the sausage gravy.

With the sausage cooked, Sierra drained the grease and added flour to make a roux. She remembered her mom watching her like a hawk. "Stir, Sierra, keep stirring and bringing the temperature up," she could hear her mom saying.

However, Sierra didn't burn the roux and added the sausage to blend the ingredients before the biscuit timer beeped. With breakfast ready, she set the table as Ruth and Luke came through the front door. The savory smell of biscuits brought back fond memories of having breakfast with their parents. A welcome distraction for the morning.

While the breakfast triggered thoughts of happier times, they sat down at the table to enjoy the sunrise and catch their breath. Luke gathered his gear and guns to leave an hour before he needed to arrive at the hangar. He allowed extra time to perform more checks with Wes lurking around.

"Need anything before I go?"

His sisters shook their heads and waved goodbye.

With Luke en route to the hangar, the two proceeded to review the assessment. Sierra pulled up Google Earth and begun exploring hypothetical scenarios with Ruth when they heard a knock at the door. Ruth drew her pistol and approached the door. She recognized the truck as she peered from the window. In haste, Sierra gathered the papers and maps and stowed them as Ruth opened the door. "Hi, Dirk. Please come in."

Sierra grabbed a seat next to Ruth, and Dirk clasped his hands. He took a deep breath and paused. "Wes's cellmate shared some information with me. He knew your dad and out of respect for him, he couldn't sit on it. Wes is planning to torture you and livestream the event, Sierra. He wants to skin you alive. You know I will not stand by, so how can I help?"

Without saying a word, Sierra pulled out her phone and showed him the picture of Teddy and the note.

"Wes did this?"

Sierra nodded with a sidelong glance.

Dirk shook his head. "I could arrest him if you want, but I realize you can handle this on your own. Although I won't ask for details, call me if you need help to block off roads or anything. I mean it, anything."

"Thank you, Dirk. We appreciate it. Keep your burner phone on."

"Of course," he said as he waved goodbye and headed out the door. Once Dirk drove out of their driveway, Ruth looked at Sierra with watchful eyes as she leaned in.

"Are you all right?"

Sierra had turned white as a ghost. "I'm okay. It's a lot to come to terms with when you hear someone wants to skin you alive and livestream the event."

"I won't let him hurt you. It ends tonight," Ruth said as she hugged her. She understood the limits of planning. Her intuition was by far one of the best defenses against Wes. Ruth was on high alert and watching the animals for signs because most times, they knew before she did.

※ ※ ※

While Ruth and Sierra held down the ranch and prepared for battle, Luke and Jake flew over Baldy Peak in search of Tristan.

Once airborne, Luke observed Jake. The corners of his mouth turned down as he interlaced his fingers.

"What is he wearing?"

"A bright blue fleece jacket with a yellow baseball cap, jeans, and hiking boots."

As they continued flying over the area, Luke caught a flash of silver out of the corner of his eye. "Wait. That looks like a space blanket at eleven o'clock."

Luke circled the hiker for a closer look. They could see the hiker waving them on with his space blanket.

"That's Tristan, and he's hiking out." Relief swept over the cockpit. Luke took the coordinates of Tristan's location on his tablet for reference, then they flew toward the trailhead, tipping their wing before returning to the hangar.

"I worried about what we'd find," Jake said, his voice trembling.

Luke put his hand on Jake's shoulder.

The rest of the trip remained quiet, with Jake reflecting on recent events. Luke began radio communications with Air Traffic Control to prepare for landing back at the hangar. Once they were back, Jake approached Luke.

"Thank you for helping me find Tristan." Jake paused for a few moments. "Another thing has been bothering me. It's about Sierra. Someone wants to do her harm."

"Yesterday, her stalker was released from prison. And this morning, she found one of her barn cats dead with a threatening note written in blood."

"That's serious. I'll be in Telford. Call me for anything."

"Thanks, Jake. We have plans for Wes," he said, walking over to the trucks.

Luke scanned both of their vehicles for trackers and other devices, and then he hugged him and they were on their way.

DARCY MCDANIEL

✷ ✷ ✷

Luke was on edge. He disliked leaving his sisters alone with Wes on the loose. He called Ruth from his burner and sensed concern in her voice. His breathing was fast yet shallow as he gasped for air. She mentioned Dirk stopped by with news about Wes that was better shared in person. Luke sailed down the road, burning the breeze to return to the ranch.

It was around one o'clock in the afternoon. Bone-chilling feelings washed over Luke as he approached the driveway, goosebumps racing up his arms. An owl flew in front of his truck and locked eyes with him. Her piercing gaze bored into his soul, leaving him feeling raw and exposed.

When he drove up to the house, it was like he was moving in slow motion. His heart raced as he got out of the truck, grabbed his gun, and walked inside. He found blood and drag marks, though Trixie and Koda were okay. "What the hell happened here?"

Luke's eyes bulged as he assessed the scene. His stomach churned.

Ruth cleared her throat and Luke whirled with his gun drawn.

She held up her hands. "Don't shoot, Luke. It's me."

Luke lowered his gun and hugged her. "I was so worried about what I'd find inside."

"Wes is in the shop." Ruth put her hand on Luke's shoulder, and he took a deep breath. She mentioned she wanted to tackle the stains on the wood floors before they set. Luke exhaled, the air whistled across his lips as he clutched his chest.

MOUNTAIN OF SECRETS

With cleaning gloves in hand and her caddy of cleaners, Ruth evaluated the kitchen and entryway, wearing her hazmat suit. As a mist of chemicals coated the floor, Ruth began cleaning the stains before heading to the shop. Meanwhile, he acknowledged her and walked outside to his truck. After he pulled his truck around, Luke joined Sierra.

On a whim, Ruth went to the front porch and noticed a white vehicle crawling along the road. She dashed into the house and grabbed the binos, then hurried back to the porch to get a better look. Through the binos, she saw a middle-aged woman driving a white Subaru Forester with bright orange New York plates. "That's odd. I suppose no stranger than me glassing the road wearing a hazmat suit," she said, a playful glint in her eye, her voice barely above a whisper. Her neck hair prickled like a signal flare as she stared at the driver. After grabbing the cell phone from her pocket, she took a picture of the vehicle and jotted down its details for reference.

When Luke arrived at the shop, it was an ominous scene. He saw Wes tied to a metal folding chair sitting atop a plastic drop cloth. Wes was fading out of consciousness, and Luke noticed a deep gash on his arm, which explained the blood in the kitchen. Ruth and Sierra had arranged the plastic cloth with the chair offset from a corner to make it easier to wrap the body.

Soon, Ruth arrived, wearing her hazmat suit with her caddy in hand. She looked at Sierra and then Luke like Tony Soprano conducting business with a nod.

The tension in the shop was a level twelve on a scale of one to ten. Sierra walked up to Wes and splashed cold water on his face to wake him. It looked like she had awoken a monster; his eyes burned with hatred. She paused before speaking. "All right, Wes, let's discuss. Why did you target me?"

Wes spat on her. Without an ounce of emotion, Sierra wiped the spit off her face and unfolded her knife. With an icy look, she stabbed him in the stomach, careful to avoid vital organs, but pushing deep enough to hurt. He winced in pain and squirmed in the chair.

Sierra glared at Wes. "You're not leaving here alive, so you choose whether this goes fast, by bullet, or slow, by a thousand cuts. If you answer truthfully, this process will be over soon." Her stern voice sliced through any hopes Wes had of leaving there alive.

Wes flared his nostrils and gritted his teeth. "Because you were vulnerable."

"Do you regret killing Zeke Adams?"

He shook his head.

"Why do you want to kill me?" Sierra locked eyes with Wes like she was searching for meaning.

"You rejected me like everyone else in my life and I snapped."

"I heard you wanted to skin me alive and livestream it? Why?"

Wes's face blushed. "For the shock factor; I was in prison with a reputation to uphold."

"Do you have any last words?"

"No, let's get it over with. I'd prefer a bullet over the knife."

"This ends today, Wes. I know you won't stop, so I will stop you."

"Sierra," Wes said with labored breathing, "see you in hell."

After switching off the safety on her Colt .32 pistol, Sierra held her gun up to Wes. Hatred faded from his eyes. In one fluid movement, she pulled the trigger.

At that moment, the tension lifted. Sierra took in the scene, then wiped the blood that had sprayed onto her face. She tasted blood and wiped her mouth on her sleeve.

Next, Sierra cut the rope that secured Wes to the chair.

"Will you give me a hand lifting him out of the chair?" Sierra spoke with casualness, like she asked for help with the groceries, not lifting a body.

Luke came over after putting his gloves on and helped her lift him out of the chair and onto the plastic.

"Roll him like we're wrapping meat?"

She nodded while pulling her leather gloves tighter.

They folded the corners in and began rolling him, then used duct tape to secure the plastic.

"My plan is to go to Cutthroat Creek and bury him behind the stock water tank in the trees. Luke or Ruth, I'd appreciate it if one of you helped me?"

Before Ruth could reply, Luke blurted out, "I can go. We made a pretty good team with Nate."

"Okay, then I'll clean up around here," Ruth said.

It was now four o'clock in the afternoon, so they divvied things up. Luke hooked up the trailer, swept the vehicles for tracking and recording devices, and grabbed the shovels. Sierra caught and saddled the horses and brought her Predator long gun, ammo, and thermal binos. When Luke pulled around with the trailer, Sierra finished saddling Misty and stroked her mane, which glistened in the sun.

Luke hopped out of the truck and opened the trailer gate. Sierra noticed the front divider was closed and she could see plastic. "Ruth helped me load him and I threw in some fencing supplies for good measure."

Sierra raised her eyebrows. "Good call, Luke."

With the horses loaded, Luke secured the trailer gate and saw Ruth walking down when he looked up.

"I packed you both a meal, headlamps, and some disinfecting wipes. Be careful and don't take chances. I'll let Jake and Dirk know that we've neutralized the threat," she said.

"Thank you, Ruth," Sierra said, with emotion dripping from her voice.

Ruth waved goodbye while Luke and Sierra used the wipes before pulling out of the driveway. She swished water in her mouth to get rid of the taste of blood. The smell of bean burritos wafted through the cab as they bolted down the dirt road. "Let's save these for later," Luke said, fighting off dry heaves. A sea of dust followed the truck and trailer on the dry summer day.

★ ★ ★

While Luke and Sierra headed out to Cutthroat Creek with their perishable cargo, Ruth grabbed her 30-06 rifle, binos, and ghillie suit. She couldn't shake the feeling about the woman in the Subaru. Putting her gun on the rack of the four-wheeler, she drove to a vantage point and surveyed the area. Within a few minutes, she located the Subaru hidden in a patch of trees off the road about four hundred yards from her location.

The woman stood outside and flipped through papers on the hood of her car. Ruth's posture became rigid when she saw the woman load a 9mm. With the 15x magnification on her binos, Ruth saw the pictures of her and her siblings. "That's no coincidence," she said, gathering her gear and rushing back to the house.

When she arrived, she threw the items into her truck and headed toward Cutthroat Creek to catch up with Luke and Sierra. "I don't trust that woman," she said, clenching the steering wheel.

✱ ✱ ✱

After they turned onto the main dirt road, Luke looked at Sierra. "Do you feel relieved?"

"Yes, I'm glad he's gone," she said as her voice trailed off.

After several minutes of silence, Luke re-engaged the conversation. "How did things unfold with Wes?"

"Not as I expected. Ruth suggested we get ready, so we were in the shop, putting the plastic drop cloth in place. Right when I set the chair down, I received an alert on my phone. It was Wes at the front door. While Ruth distracted him, I came in from behind, held a knife to his throat, and whispered in his ear to drop to his knees. Wes struggled for the knife and I slashed his arm. Ruth hit him over the head with a bookend and knocked him out, then we loaded him into the truck and drove into the shop."

"Way to handle the situation. Did he walk out to the ranch or drive part way, then walk?"

"I'm not sure. Ruth planned to inform Dirk about seeing his truck around our place, though."

Luke and Sierra reflected on the gravity of the situation. While they made their way to Cutthroat Creek, the sun's rays felt intense, beating down on them. Sierra's cell phone rang; it was Ruth. "You're on speaker."

Her voice gained a couple of octaves. "Look for a white Subaru Forester with New York plates. She's after us... Take her..." There was a lot of static and they lost the call.

Luke jerked his head toward Sierra. "Ruth sounded serious."

"Let's proceed with caution here," she said as her electric blue eyes scanned the landscape. Her cell phone rang, and it startled her. It was Dirk. "Take the pullout ahead where we meet Dirk. The reception is spotty, but we might have a bar of service there."

"Okay, hang on for a bumpy ride," Luke said as the trailer bounced and squeaked over ruts in the dirt road.

After several attempts, she connected with Dirk. "You're scratchy, but I can hear you."

"Wes missed roll call at the halfway house. He's on the run, so be on guard. Let's meet..." She lost the call but relayed the update to Luke.

"Well, that didn't take long to figure out he's missing," Luke said, grinding his teeth.

Long sighs filled the cab as a fly buzzed their heads.

After a few moments, they got back on the road. The trailer rattled like a shaker deck.

Before they turned off to Cutthroat Creek, a woman standing beside a white Subaru Forester flagged them down. Luke slowed down and greeted her. "Hi," the motorist said, a middle-aged woman in her late forties with shoulder-length wavy gray hair. She waved her hands in front of her face to fan the dust away.

"Hello, can we help you?"

"Yes, I'm visiting from New York, and I wanted to tag along with some real-life cowboys," she said. "It's for a book I'm writing about the Wild West."

"We'd love to help you out, but we're in a hurry. A calf has fallen into a hole and needs our help."

"Oh, wonderful, that'd be great."

"We might have to put him down, depending on his condition."

The woman seemed put off.

Luke wished her a great day and went down the road.

"That was close. Time to leave: 9mm with a suppressor on her seat. I bet she's the woman Ruth warned us about."

"Do you think she has ulterior motives?"

"We'll find out."

Sierra shifted in her seat. "I believe we're becoming desensitized to violence."

He noticed an uneasiness in her voice. "I wonder that, too," Luke said as he stared into the horizon. When he checked his mirrors, he noticed headlights.

"Oh shit, it's the white Subaru again. I'll pull over at the next turn and let you out. I need you to take out the driver's side front tire, so it'll pull her down over the bank. If the crash doesn't kill her, finish her," Luke said.

"Copy," Sierra said. While showing vulnerability in one moment, she became a tactical operator in the next.

In a flash, Sierra grabbed her long gun, bailed out of the vehicle, and dove into the trees. Sierra posted up, assessed her shot, and dialed in her long gun. She could see Luke stopped above the next corner, right as the Subaru poured it on. Slowing her breathing, she positioned herself for the shot at five hundred yards.

Three, two, one, *pow*! Sierra hit her target, and the Subaru careened off the road and over the bank. It rolled four times, ejecting the woman before hanging up on a tree. Sierra grabbed her casing and left her post, making her way down the bank and picking her route with caution.

When she arrived, the woman, impaled on a broken tree, clung to life.

"Who sent you?"

"You'll never know."

"Enlighten me, or your final breaths will surpass your current agony." Sierra twisted her mangled arm, and the woman groaned.

"Dell Teague," the woman said, struggling for air. She gasped for her final breath.

Sierra couldn't believe what she heard, and she slapped herself to snap out of it.

Dell Teague's father Wayne battled Grandpa Sig over Sally Worthers. Wayne disappeared, and Grandpa Sig married Sally. The bad blood between the Teagues and the LaRaes originated with Wayne and Sig and continued through the generations.

"Rest in peace," Sierra said, assessing the scene.

Despite a five-star crash test rating, the Subaru Forester looked the worse for wear. Blood and car parts littered the scene. Sierra worked with speed and precision to find the woman's personal items among the wreckage.

The sun peeked through the trees as Sierra scanned the area. Within minutes, she grabbed a camera, a cell phone, and a 9mm, and she beat feet out of there, using a branch to sweep her tracks. She could hear a truck with a trailer lumbering along. Sierra climbed to the road and hopped in with Luke. Next, she took a waypoint of the crash on her phone. They agreed to get back in service and call Ruth and Dirk.

A few minutes down the road, Sierra noticed Ruth's truck approaching.

Luke stopped on the side of the road, and Ruth pulled up alongside him.

"Have you seen the woman in the white Forester?"

"We've seen her, all right. Sierra shot her front tire to force her over the bank. The crash ejected her and impaled her on to a tree. How'd you know about the woman?"

"When cleaning the kitchen, I stepped on the porch and noticed a white Subaru Forester with New York plates. I glassed her in the binos after you left and saw she was looking at our photos on the hood of her car, so I got in my truck and called you."

"You're uncanny, Ruth."

Ruth's eyes widened as she bit her cheek.

Sierra sent Ruth the coordinates and got out of the truck with the camera, 9mm, and cell phone. "The woman said Dell Teague sent her."

"Dell Teague? Jeez. I called Dirk, and he's on his way. I'll send him the coordinates and then head back to the ranch."

With a baffled look, Sierra addressed Ruth and Luke. "I'm confused. Didn't Dell lose his faculties with the last stroke?"

"That's what I thought. Although he might be more capable than he leads people to believe."

Luke shook his head in skepticism at the latest twist in the Teague saga.

After the brief detour, Luke and Sierra returned to their purpose of the trip: Burying Wes. One wrecked Subaru and one deceased hit woman later, they waved as Ruth sped down the road. Luke swung wide to go toward the mountains.

Upon their arrival at Cutthroat Creek, the sun rallied on the horizon. A deep amber hue illuminated the meadow. Sierra and Luke exchanged glances. She pulled on her gloves and then stepped out of the truck. They agreed to ride double and haul Wes on Lucky, since he'd hauled game animals.

Sierra brought Lucky around the truck to load up the gear and store her long gun. She also secured the shovels to her saddle. An eagle screeched above and Sierra scanned the sky. She stepped into a spiderweb while watching the eagle and brushed it off her face.

Lucky in position, they counted to three and heaved Wes out of the trailer. Even with gloves, the plastic slipped in their hands when they carried him.

Once they re-positioned, they hoisted Wes over the saddle, so he lay sideways. Luke tightened his cinches, then swung his leg over the saddle. Next, Sierra sprang up behind Luke and straddled his saddle.

She looked back at Wes. The obsessed man who stalked Sierra like an animal lay rolled in plastic on a horse awaiting burial by moonlight. Yet the end of Wes Wood brought closure to Sierra and her siblings. Wes terrorized not only Sierra, but Luke and Ruth, too. His single pursuit of revenge was no match for a family forged by tragedy. To the LaRaes, there were no limits because family meant forever.

The light breeze rattled the plastic-wrapped corpse as a skunk trotted in front of Misty. She took a wide berth to avoid the skunk and hugged the trees out to the stock water tank. Once they reached the tank, Luke cut west, deeper into the trees, and Sierra guided him to the burial site. A family of raccoons growled from behind a clump of trees, and watched their every move.

When they arrived at the location, Sierra dismounted Misty, followed by Luke, and he secured Misty to a tree and loosened the cinches. As the daylight waned, they unloaded Wes close to his burial site. Sierra adjusted the cinches on the saddle while Luke removed the shovels and handed her one. A chorus of animals scurrying and crashing through the brush filled Cutthroat Creek, intersected by shovels clanking and wolves howling. An owl hooted from above where they were working. Luke looked up at the owl, feeling his judging eyes.

Within two hours, they completed digging the grave. Sierra suggested they burn the plastic in case there were fingerprints, so they cut the plastic off Wes. After they rolled it up, they placed it in the grave before lighting it with

Sierra's lighter. They moved upwind of the smoke to avoid the chemicals and stench. When the plastic consumed, they lowered Wes into the grave. Peering into the grave, they looked down at his pale, limp body.

Luke and Sierra paid their respects and grabbed their shovels. Next, they scooped the dirt back into the grave in quick order. They were sweating and the light breeze created an eerie chill in the air. Cutthroat Creek's darkness thrived at night. Whether ghosts, lost souls, or predators, a haunting quality pervaded the area.

A shiver ran up Sierra's spine. She paused when she looked at him.

"I'll finish here. Will you grab the ammo can?" Luke nodded.

He grabbed his shovel and headed about thirty yards away before she heard the clattering of metal against rock. Luke removed the ammo can, filled the hole with dirt, and rejoined Sierra. After another search of the area, they found nothing remaining. Next, they tightened their cinches and got back on their saddles.

Luke and Sierra checked both stock water tanks, finding them up and running. They grabbed the binos to scan the area for predators. Sierra spotted a wolf pack six hundred yards east of their location, feasting on an elk carcass. However, the cattle congregated in the trees seemed unbothered. Bats screeched by, their sounds cutting through the silence. Tilting their heads to determine their location, they surveyed the area one last time before returning to the truck.

Sierra's mind raced. *Did Dell Teague plan this retaliation before his last stroke, or are Nate's siblings more involved in the family business than they initially thought?* The only thing she knew: Her family would be ready for the next round.

As the near-full moon illuminated their way to the truck, the two silhouettes danced in the dark, with a ghastly aura surrounding them, like headless horsemen. With the wolves howling in the distance, a single lonesome call stood out above the rest. Luke held the reins tighter with a grim look and sunken eyes. "You think we'll get a break from all of the action for a while?" he said as he gestured with his fingers.

"No," Sierra said with a hollowness in her voice. "We're just getting started."

ACKNOWLEDGMENTS

To **Mike Waitz**: thank you for being a wellspring of light during the editing process. To my readers: I hope this book brings you as much joy to read as it has brought me to write. If this story resonates with you, kindly consider leaving a review on Amazon to help others discover its magic.

ABOUT THE AUTHOR

DARCY MCDANIEL is a former hotshot firefighter who now ignites her passion for storytelling from the tranquil landscapes of rural North Central Washington. When she's not helping her family on their ranch, she's writing thrillers with a flair for the cowboy lifestyle. Darcy finds inspiration in the great outdoors and craves rugged places where trees outnumber people. Follow her writing journey as she seamlessly blends her love for nature with unpredictable plot twists that leap off the page at darcymcdaniel.com.

Ready for the next book in the Legacy Series? Find exclusive updates at darcymcdaniel.com.

Made in the USA
Columbia, SC
02 January 2025